CONTENTS

Ice Dreams

Ice Dreams

Beverly Scudamore

James Lorimer & Company Ltd., Publishers
Toronto

James Lorimer & Company Ltd. acknowledges the support of the Ontario Arts Council. We acknowledge the support of the Government of Canada through the Book Publishing Industry Development Program (BPIDP) for our publishing activities. We acknowledge the support of the Canada Council for the Arts for our publishing program. We acknowledge the support of the Government of Ontario through the Ontario Media Development Corporation's Ontario Book Initiative.

Cover illustration: James Bentley

Library and Archives Canada Cataloguing in Publication

Scudamore, Beverly, 1956–
Ice dreams

(Sports stories ; 65)
ISBN 10: 1-55028-813-X ISBN 13: 978-1-55028-813-1 (bound)

ISBN 10: 1-55028-812-1 ISBN 13: 978-1-55028-812-4 (pbk.)

I. Title. II. Series: Sports stories (Toronto, Ont.); 65.

PS8587.C82I24 2003 jC813'.54 C2003-904181-6

James Lorimer & Co. Ltd,
Publishers
317 Adelaide Street West,
Suite 1002
Toronto, Ontario
M5V 1P9
www.lorimer.ca

Distributed in the United States by:
Orca Book Publishers
P.O. Box 468
Custer, WA USA
98240-0468

Printed and bound in Canada.

For John

1 Under the Sea

Blue floodlights shone across the ice surface creating the illusion of a calm ocean. Along the boards, crêpe paper fish swam through strands of silvery seaweed. Except for the rhythmic sound of waves rolling out of the audio system, the Linton Heights Arena was silent as the audience awaited the first skaters.

The King Neptune Waltz began to play as a cloud of jellyfish floated onto the ice. The crowd rose to their feet whistling and clapping for the group of toddlers dressed in puffy layers of white chiffon. Next came the clownfish, performing silly antics — when they weren't busy picking jellyfish off the ice.

Just my luck, I thought. I get scheduled to follow the most popular act in the ice carnival. What twelve-year-old can compete with a bunch of baby-faced jellyfish who can't even stand up on ice?

I adjusted my long, pointy hat, its weight feeling strange on my head. Then, without warning, my skin started to tingle and burn. I wiggled in my tight costume, trying to get comfortable, but the sensation grew worse. It felt as if a million fire ants were crawling all over my body, tickling me with their toes and nipping at my flesh.

I turned to Jill, the seahorse, who was standing behind me in line. "Scratch my back! Hurry, before I go crazy."

She held up her hands. "Sorry, Maya, I'm stuck. These gloves fit like glue."

I looked around in desperation.

Before I perform, I get prickly bumps all over my skin if I feel nervous. The doctor calls it urticaria. I get the same reaction when I make a speech at school. Some people start to shake when they get stressed; some cry; others make a dash for the washroom. I get itchy.

More than anything, I needed to get to the dressing room where I had left my anti-itch spray in my skating bag. With only three minutes to go before my solo performance, I bolted from the line. As I rounded the corner in the hallway, I felt a firm grip on my arm.

"Where are you going, Maya?"

My coach, Natasha Shishkova, loomed over me, waggling an accusing finger in my face. "Tsk, tsk, tsk," she said in her thick, Russian accent. "Trying to escape?"

"No! I-I just need my spray."

"There is no time!" She grabbed my chin, tilting my head upwards until we were eye to eye. "All great skaters get nervous," she said, pinning me under her stare. "It's what gives you 'the edge.'" She placed an arm on my shoulder and I felt myself sinking under her weight. "Now, go out there," she said. "Kick your butt."

"You mean 'kick some butt,'" I corrected her.

"Yes, that too," she said.

Coach is a big woman. She used to compete on the Russian team in pair skating, which is hard to believe considering that her legs are as thick as tree trunks. In pair skating, the guy must be able to lift the girl over his head. It was easy to picture Natasha picking up a guy, but who could pick up her? Jill told me that Natasha wasn't always so big — she looked like a twig in old photos. One thing is for sure, Natasha's size alone commanded our respect.

Gripping my arm, Natasha escorted me to the head of the line up. When the lights dimmed, she nudged me onto the ice. I skated to the middle of the rink. There, I struck my pose under a spotlight, positioning my arms and legs at forty-five degree angles so that my shape resembled a starfish. My skating dress shimmered gold, as did my tights and pointy hat. The opening bars to the Spunky Starfish began to play. Taking a deep breath, I reminded myself it would all be over soon.

I loosened up by performing a few simple spins

and turns. Then, in time to the music, I took off into the air for a half rotation, easily completing the waltz jump. So far, so good. But my program was about to become more challenging. Next, I did a difficult combination of jumps, getting good height and smooth landings. No time to celebrate, for the double Axel was still ahead. Never before had I performed this move in front of an audience. For that matter, I had only just been able to get it right. Besides, how could I concentrate when my skin was waging war against me? Despite all my arguments, Natasha insisted I was ready to try it.

The music grew louder, climbing toward the dramatic crescendo when (if all went as planned) I would be completing two-and-a-half rotations in the air.

The audience was hushed. I could feel their eyes fixed upon me. There was no turning back. I skated powerfully, pushing up into the air to complete one full rotation. My head was high, my body spinning … but something felt wrong …

My timing was off. I was rotating too fast and losing control. Smack! I felt the pain as my body slid across the ice and heard the audience gasp. Then there was silence. I lay still on the ice for a moment. That's what real starfish do anyway … laze about the ocean floor. They don't go around performing double Axels.

A loud rat-a-tat-tat on the glass demanded my attention. I looked up and saw my father motioning for me to get up. I could read his lips. "Arriba! Arriba!" he was calling in Spanish.

Falling is a part of figure skating. We never get used to the pain of landing on ice — it feels like hitting cement. The best a skater can hope for is to learn not to cry.

The crowd remained silent. I lifted myself off the ice, feeling an ache in my left side. But like all trained skaters, I knew "the show must go on." Pasting a smile on my face, I lapped the rink.

"This one is for you, Mom," I said, before I took off. One rotation ... two rotations ... I smiled inside for this time I knew I was going to nail the double Axel. Another half rotation and I landed smoothly on the ice. Yes!

I held my head high to the sound of loud applause and cheers.

The lights dimmed and the carefree music took on a menacing tone. A grey shark glided onto the ice. Matt Gagnon's head poked out from a set of toothy jaws. I could hear little kids' screams mixed with terror and delight. A wild chase ensued — the helpless starfish flitting and spinning while the angry shark performed a series of twists and leaps in hot pursuit. When the shark finally cornered the starfish, it looked like the end — until that amazing superstar — me! — leaped out of the predator's bloodthirsty jaws, slid under a fin, and escaped out the exit.

As I headed to the dressing room, the other skaters congratulated me. Natasha grabbed my hand and squeezed hard. "Way to go! A gold medal performance."

I rolled my eyes. "I over-rotated the double axel."

She led me back to the gate. "Listen to the crowd," she said. "They are your judges tonight."

I had to admit: all that cheering and clapping did make me feel good.

In the dressing room I peeled off my skating dress and hung it neatly on the costume rack. Natasha goes berserk if we leave the delicate costumes lying around, since a lot of time and money goes into sewing the outfits.

When I removed my hat, my hair spilled down my back in long coils. My hair is naturally curly — with ringlets — and it's always a bit messy, even after I comb it. My best friend, Yin Li, is totally jealous of my hair. That's so weird because I wish I had her straight black hair. It glows like the sun, and there is never a strand out of place. Even after a roller coaster ride, Yin's hair falls right back into place.

Before I pulled on my jeans and sweater, I checked my skin. All that was left of the urticaria was a rash of tiny, red pin-pricks. It was strange how the hot, prickly sensation could come and go so fast.

Remembering that Yin and my dad were saving me a seat at the show, I quickly packed my skating bag, threw it over my shoulder, and ran upstairs to find them. A few minutes later, I plopped down on a padded seat next to Yin. "Where's Dad?" I asked.

"He'll be right back," she said. "He went to get something."

"So … whad'ya think? My routine was pretty lame, eh?"

She hit me with a bag of popcorn. "What do you mean? You were awesome!"

"Ever see a shark chase a starfish? I don't think so. Anyway, it doesn't matter. I'm done." I grabbed a handful of hot, buttered popcorn and stuffed it in my mouth.

"You had such a great season," Yin said, "learning the double Axel and medalling at two competitions. At the rate you are going, you will be unstoppable next year."

I stopped chewing and repeated, "I am done … finished!"

"No way! You have been skating ever since you were three. You can't just quit. Besides, what would your dad say?"

I grabbed another handful of popcorn. "Dad actually believes I am going to make the Olympic team. That is such a laugh. Taylor Wellington and Kelly Brice are members of the elite squad. They train twenty hours a week. They take ballet lessons to improve their flexibility and balance. Those are the girls Natasha is developing for the Olympics, not me!"

"If you train more often, you could be just as good,"Yin insisted.

Yin was such a good friend, always supporting me.

"Maybe — with the help of a truck load of money," I said. "But it's more than that. Natasha says you must want the Olympics with all your heart. The truth is, I don't. It's not even close to what I want."

"Well, what ..."

"Magnífico!" A familiar hand squeezed my shoulder. "You were wonderful, tonight, Chiquita." Dad slipped into the seat beside me. He handed me a single pink rose, and for a moment, I truly felt like a star. Then Dad leaned to the woman next to him. "This is my daughter, the starfish," he said, gesturing my way.

The woman smiled. "Nice to meet you. I enjoyed your performance very much."

"Thanks," I mumbled.

Dad couldn't leave it at that. "Maya is only twelve years old. Don't be surprised if you see her in the next Olympics."

"That is wonderful, dear," she said. "Imagine, an Olympian from the city of Linton."

I elbowed Dad. "You're embarrassing me."

"What do you mean?" he said, holding his hand over his heart. "Where I grew up in Mexico there was no such thing as an ice rink. Chiquita, I am proud of you. I want to show you off to the world."

I stared at the ice. "Don't."

The opening bars to the Dance of the Dolphins caught my attention. Taylor Wellington glided gracefully onto the ice. Her long, blonde hair was pulled back, and she wore a royal blue costume. Natasha had awarded Taylor the role of the dolphin because she could perform the triple lutz, one of the most difficult jumps in figure skating. Taylor opened her performance with some tricky footwork, followed by a combination of jumps. When she began skating backward crossovers, I knew she was about to attempt the triple lutz. Suddenly, she took off high into the air, completing three full rotations, and landing smoothly. The audience rose to their feet cheering, and I joined in with a loud burst of whistles.

Once the applause had died, Yin elbowed me. "So, if you don't want to figure skate anymore, what do you want to do?"

I answered with a shrug.

She wouldn't let it go. "Tell me your deepest desires … all your wildest dreams."

Yin cracked me up with her drama queen routine. "Maybe I'll play hockey with you."

"Are you serious?"

"I can picture it now: Maya Sanchez spins up the ice, leaps over the defense, and scores the winning goal." I let out a sigh. "Yeah, it would be fun."

I glanced over at Dad. He was leaning forward in his chair intently watching the skaters. What were the chances he would let me quit figure skating, and sign me up for hockey?

Get real! I told myself. It will never happen.

2 From Cooties to Cuties

Boing … Boing … Boing …"

I whirled around in my desk, glaring at Todd Marshall. His greasy hair was glued to his head. A yellow, crusty stain was smeared across his sweatshirt. My guess is he had eaten runny eggs for breakfast. But what really grossed me out were his fingernails; they were black with grunge.

I curled my lips back into a snarl. "Don't touch my hair!"

"Man, those are crazy coils," he said, yanking on another one.

"Leave them alone!" I warned.

"These would make a great science fair entry: 'Unravelling the mystery of the coil.'"

"Back off, Toad!"

"Make me."

Okay, I said to myself. You asked for it.

When the teacher looked the other way, I leaned

over the side of my desk, holding my stomach and moaning. In obvious pain, I turned to Todd and mumbled, "Are you feeling okay?"

A deep line creased his forehead. "Yeah, why?"

Rising up in my desk like a cobra snake, I glared down my nose at him. Then I spit my venom: "Because you're making me sick."

Stung him, I told myself — until I realized he was laughing. He thought my insult was hilarious.

"Maya Sanchez!" the teacher snapped. "Face the front and let Todd Marshall do his work."

The class turned, curious to see what was going on between us. I shoved my fingers down my throat to make sure no one got the wrong impression.

Grade six is almost over, I reminded myself. With any luck, the Toad won't be in my class next year.

Taking my protractor out of my desk, I read the instructions on my math worksheet: Measure and identify the following angles. I began to measure an obtuse angle.

Brooke Miller slipped me a note on her way to the pencil sharpener. In blue marker, she had written: "Awesome news! Hope we get to play on the same team. HOCKEY RULES!!!"

I looked over at Brooke. She shot me a thumbs-up. Amanda Neal was standing in line behind Brooke. She gave me a knowing smile. Then, pretending she was holding a hockey stick, she wound up and took a slap shot. Dancing on the spot, she mouthed, "She shoots, she scores!"

All of a sudden, I felt sick to my stomach — this time for real! The night before, at the ice carnival, I hadn't actually been serious about playing hockey. Sure, it would be fun, but ...

When the recess bell rang, I cornered Yin at her locker. "You told everyone!"

"I couldn't help it," she said, grabbing her blue jacket. "I was so excited."

"But I'm not even sure if ..."

Her jaw dropped. "Didn't you mean it?"

"It's not that," I said. "I think hockey is cool. It's just ..."

Out of the corner of my eye, I noticed Todd walking in my direction. He had a soccer ball tucked under his arm. As he approached, his eyes narrowed. "Is your face hurting you?" he asked, looking concerned.

I touched my cheeks. "No, why?"

"'Cuz it's killing me." He bounced the ball off my shoulder. "Get it?"

I clenched my teeth. "Yeah, I get it — and now you're going to get it!"

Leaving Yin at her locker, I took off through the halls of Linton Valley School chasing Todd. He managed to deke around a class of kindergartners who were lined up at the doors waiting to be allowed outside for recess. When I tried to follow, the teacher called out, "Stop right there, young lady. No running in the halls!"

By the time I made it through the doors, Todd had disappeared into the schoolyard. Determined to find him, I checked the climbers, and then headed over to the basketball hoops. No sign of him. Wandering out to the field, I scanned the baseball diamond and soccer field.

"Who are you looking for?"

I jumped back. Brooke had managed to sneak up on me. "No one," I replied, quickly.

Just then, Yin came running across the field. "Did you get Todd?" she called out.

Way to go, Yin, I thought. Nice timing.

Smirking, Brooke pointed to the soccer field. "He'll be somewhere in the middle of the boy's soccer game." Her green eyes sparkled with interest. "Why do you care?"

"I … uh …"

Yin came to my rescue. "He's been getting on Maya's case," she explained.

"Yeah," I added, "he was acting like a moron — pulling out my hair and hitting me with a soccer ball."

"Hmmm …" Brooke tossed her strawberry blonde hair over her shoulders. "Sounds like Todd is in stage one."

"Stage one?" I repeated.

She grinned. "Do I have to spell it out? He's got a crush on you."

I folded my arms. "No way! Todd is gross."

"It makes sense," Brooke went on. "Some guys act gross to get a girl's attention. Craig Adams gave me a bubble gum sculpture when he liked me last summer."

"Ew," I moaned, "slime art."

"And there's burping," Yin offered. "Matt Gagnon can burp out the entire alphabet."

"He can also burp in French," I added. Secretly, I was impressed.

"Guys do clue in … eventually," Brooke said. "That's stage two."

I eyed Brooke suspiciously. "Where'd you get this 'stages' stuff?"

"My older sister, Jewel. She's got a whole stack of teen magazines."

Hmmm … Brooke had done her research.

"Don't be too hard on Todd," she went on. "He can't help it."

I rolled my eyes. "Why, 'cuz he's, like, so immature?" My teeth started to chatter. After all, it was only the beginning of April, and I had run outside in my T-shirt. But I couldn't go get my jacket; this conversation was way too interesting.

Brooke poked a zit on her chin. "It's hormones. You know … puberty. It makes boys act weird."

Yin pulled us into a private circle. "Remember when the public health nurse gave our class 'the talk'? The boys sure were quiet that day — except for Craig who was snickering and making faces."

"We weren't exactly comfortable,"Yin said.

Suddenly, I pulled away from the circle. "Whatever! All I know is you won't see me acting stupid around a guy!"

Brooke grinned. "We'll see about that."

By the time the bell rang, I had caught a major chill. All we had done the whole recess was stand around and talk about boys. What a waste. Still, I couldn't stop thinking about what Brooke had said. What if Todd really did like me?

At lunch, I got my answer. I was eating a bologna and cheese sandwich when Todd hit me on the shoulder with an eraser. "Amanda says you are going to play hockey next year. Is it true?"

A thought flashed through my head: is Todd one of the boys who Amanda phones? "I'm thinking about it," I said.

"My rep team is second place in the whole league," he said. Just then, his face lit up. "Hey, wanna see something?"

I shrugged. "Sure, why not."

I took a bite of my sandwich while Todd fumbled around in his lunch box. Eventually, he brought out two red licorices and proceeded to bite the ends off. Then he shoved a piece up each nostril and began humming a tune through his nose and right out the end of the licorices. It sounded like a kazoo. And Todd looked like a walrus with red tusks. Suddenly I cracked up.

He removed the licorices and smiled proudly. "Want one?"

"Gross!" I slapped them out of his hands.

Then it hit me ... maybe Brooke was right. Maybe Todd did like me.

★ ★ ★

That night I sat on my bedroom carpet, stretching out my muscles. They were still tight after the carnival, especially on the side that had crashed onto the ice. While I was stretching my quadriceps, the large muscles in my thighs, I stared at the picture of Mom hanging on my wall. She was a teenager, then. Her sandy coloured hair was cut short, just above her ears. Her legs were slim, but defined by muscle. She wore a metallic blue skating dress with a silver fringe attached to the collar and around the hem of the skirt. A bronze medal hung around her neck. In the background flew the yellow, black, and red flag of Germany. She was smiling, proud to be representing Canada in the World Figure Skating Championships.

After I came out of my stretch, I lay still on the floor for a moment, my eyes closed ... remembering. I was only seven when Mom got diagnosed with cancer. I never believed she would die. After all, lots of people survive cancer. And I was too young to be without a mother.

The phone rang. "Maya," Dad called, "It's for you!"

I dashed to the phone.

Yin didn't bother with "hello." She got straight to the point. "Are you serious about playing hockey?"

"I think so … why?"

"Cuz registration for next season is this weekend," she said.

"Already? But I haven't even discussed it with my dad."

"Maybe we can play on the same team and carpool to the practices."

I hesitated. "There is also the matter of my grandparents. They pay for my figure skating lessons. I don't know if they will agree."

"You'll make it work," Yin insisted.

"But … they think …"

She cut me off. "Got to go. I have something important to do." She hung up before I had a chance to say goodbye.

What's up with her? I wondered.

Wandering into the living room, I found Dad stretched out on the couch, staring at the news. Lately, he had begun to resemble a lion. For as long as I could remember, he had worn a thick moustache; but recently, he had grown a line of dark hair along his jaw-line ending in a little goatee. My dad's full name is

Felipe Sanchez, and he grew up in a small fishing village in Mexico. His father was a fisherman and his mother sold brightly coloured baskets to the tourists in the marketplace. Today, his three brothers still live in Mexico, and Dad would be there, too, if he hadn't met a Canadian figure skater named Valerie Stuart. She was vacationing at the hotel where he worked as a chef. They met on the sea and fell in love — just like in a fairy-tale — but they got cheated out of the happy ending.

I sat on the floor and stared at the TV, listening to some reporter who was stationed in the Arctic talk about melting icebergs. A partially frozen cameraman was zooming in on a massive iceberg to capture the slow drip of melt water.

"Hey, Dad, how about we switch to a hockey game?" I suggested.

"It's 9:30," he grumbled. "Go to bed."

"But Dad … I'm not tired."

"You have school tomorrow. Go! Pronto!"

The phone rang again. When I picked up the receiver, a voice blurted, "My parents said 'yes'!"

"Yin?" I said. "Is that you?"

"Isn't that great?"

"I have no idea what you're talking about."

"That's because it is a surprise," Yin explained. "Come over after school tomorrow and you will see."

"Just tell me," I begged.

"It won't be a surprise if I tell you. You must come over."

"Oh, all right," I said, at last.

"Have you talked to your dad yet?" she asked.

"It has only been five minutes," I reminded her.

Mrs Li yelled at Yin to get off the phone, so we said a quick goodbye. I returned to my bedroom to finish my stretches, after which I easily slid into the splits. In my mind, I could hear Natasha saying: stretch slowly, hold your stretch … breathe … relax … Relax? How could I? Somehow, I had to find a way to tell Dad that figure skating was not my dream — and make him understand. After that, I would convince him to let me play hockey. The more I thought about it, hockey made perfect sense. I was already a good skater. Playing on a team with my friends would be fun. And since I wouldn't be skating solo routines, I would never break out in a rash. Switching sports would be as easy as trading skates.

3 Facing Off with Dad

After school Yin and I sat together on the bus. She kept dropping clues about the surprise that awaited me at her house. "It is something you need. It is not new. It's my brother's and ..." she added with a twinkle in her eye, "it stinks."

I turned and snarled. "What could I possibly need of your brother's that is old and stinky? It had better not be dirty underwear. Seriously, that would not be funny."

Yin started to laugh. Seemed she thought it would be hysterical.

At Yin's stop, we gathered our backpacks and filed off the bus. Then we walked two blocks to her house.

Mrs Li greeted us at the front door. "Hi!" she said. "How is Mi-ya today?"

At first I thought she was talking to Yin, but then I noticed she was looking at me.

"Fine," I replied quickly. Mrs Li knows how to speak English, but sometimes I can't understand her.

She speaks with a Chinese accent and she has an unusual way of putting sentences together.

Yin raced upstairs and I followed closely behind, bumping into her brother, Kim, on the way. When she opened her bedroom door, my mouth dropped wide open. Before me, heaped on the floor, was a bulging hockey bag with a wooden stick woven through the handles.

"Kim has outgrown his equipment," Yin explained. "My parents said you can borrow it next season. The only thing is the skates … I'm not sure if they will fit."

I hugged her hard. "You are the best!"

Yin got down on her knees and unzipped the hockey bag, exposing its treasures: pants, assorted pads, a shiny, black helmet, the arm of a green jersey, the finger of a glove and the blade of a skate.

"Go ahead," she said, smiling up at me. "Try it on."

Shrugging helplessly at Yin, I confessed, "I think I need help."

"Start with the shoulder pads," she suggested.

I rummaged through the bag until I found the shoulder pads. As I pulled them out, a rotten stench filled my nostrils. "Ew … it smells nasty in there!"

"Respect the smell," Kim yelled from the hall. "It is sacred."

I lowered my voice. "Is he kidding?"

"No," Yin said. "He actually believes the smell makes him play better."

I picked up the green jersey and took a whiff, then withered up dying on the floor. "That smell isn't sacred," I moaned, "it's lethal. Kim must have to skate hard to escape death by his own smell."

Yin plugged her nose. "Maybe that's the secret to his success."

"So," I said, getting serious. "How do you get rid of the stench?"

"Try spreading the gear outside on a nice day," Yin suggested. "The sun bakes out bad odours."

Weird, but worth a try, I thought.

Minutes later, I stood in front of Yin's mirror. Packed into a ton of padding under the green jersey, I looked like the Hulk. My feet wobbled around in skates that were a few sizes too big. I felt awkward, but I didn't care. I looked and felt like a hockey player.

Yin looked bored on the bed. "Are you hungry?" she asked.

"Starving," I said, unsnapping the helmet. As I shed the hockey gear, Yin's carpet slowly disappeared under a heap of equipment. It was strange to see her bedroom looking messy, and I laughed as she ran around collecting pieces and stuffing them back in the bag. Yin and her family are neat freaks. Throughout their home are white floors and tidy rooms that never get cluttered with junk.

After Yin and I had packed all the equipment away, we ran downstairs to the kitchen. Rifling through the cupboards, she discovered a brand new bag of Creamy Delights.

As I was curling my tongue beneath the chocolate coating to the vanilla cream in the middle, her mom called, "Mi-ya, time to go home."

I shoved the whole cookie in my mouth. "See ya tomorrow," I said. "Thanks for having me over." Crumbs fell from my mouth as I spoke. Yin scooped them up in her hands.

Yin followed me to the front door where her mother was waiting, car keys in hand, and the hockey bag at her feet.

"You like?" she said, pointing to the bag.

"Yes," I said. "Thank you very much."

"Good," she said, with a big smile. "Then you take, and I will drive you home."

"Can I pick it up in a few days?" I asked. Her smile turned upside down. "You no like?"

"No … I mean yes, I like. It's awesome. It's just that my dad doesn't …"

"Your dad no like?"

I turned to Yin. She could rescue me with a few words in Chinese, but she was having too much fun watching me try to communicate with her mother. Finally, I just threw my backpack over my shoulders, picked up the hockey bag, and followed Mrs Li to the car. I would have to talk to my dad that night.

★ ★ ★

Dad was reading the newspaper when I walked into the living room. "What is it, Chiquita?" he asked, regarding my troubled face. "School?" He promptly put down the paper and placed his reading glasses on the table.

My heart began to pound. I had rehearsed my lines until I had memorized them. There was no turning back. "Um … Dad, I have to tell you something," I began. "I've been figure skating for nine years and it has been awesome, but now I want to try something new."

I peered into Dad's dark eyes. His expression didn't change. He patted the cushion next to him, inviting me to sit down. Reluctantly, I walked over and joined him on the couch. Running his fingers through my hair, he spoke gently: "You are one of the top skaters at the Linton Heights Figure Skating Club. Your whole life you have worked hard to be the best. And Natasha has been more than a coach ever since your mother died."

"I know, Dad."

He stared hard at me, like he was searching for something in my eyes. "Perhaps a rest over the summer is all you need."

I couldn't think … couldn't breathe. I had to get some space. Standing up, I simply blurted out, "Going to the Olympics is not my dream! I am not Mom. I want to choose for myself."

I waited for him to say something, but he didn't. He looked away, and the room fell silent.

"I don't like solo competition," I said, at last. "You know I get itchy skin."

He took a deep breath and exhaled loudly. "What do you want?"

"I want to be part of a team," I said, feeling my voice gain strength. "I want to skate … and score. Dad … I want to play hockey."

His dark brows connected into a long, straight line. "No está bien! Hockey is a violent sport. Just the other night I watched the Toronto Maple Leafs play the Montreal Canadiens. They went loco smashing each other into the boards, and slashing with their sticks. I watched two fights break out."

"Women's hockey is different," I explained. "Body checking is not allowed. Yin is the smallest girl on her team, and she has never been hurt. There's no hitting in girl's hockey, not even in the Olympics. It's all about skill."

Dad didn't look convinced.

"Don't move," I said, as I headed upstairs. "I'll be right back."

A few minutes later, I returned, dragging the hockey bag behind me. "Look at all this padding," I said, laying the pieces out before him. "You could wrap me up and mail me to Mexico with all this protection."

Dad didn't laugh. "Where did this come from?" he demanded.

"Yin's brother, Kim. He outgrew it."

"So … I am the last to know," he said, his voice rising. "You told me nothing."

"Dad … it's just that … you are so proud of my figure skating. I was afraid …"

Dad looked like he was about to roar. But he didn't. Without another word, he walked out of the room. I wanted to scream at him, "You're not being fair!" But I didn't. I followed him instead — out to the kitchen where I found him sitting at the table, his head buried in his hands.

"Dad?" I said. "Are you okay?"

He gave me a faint smile and reached for my hand. "I loved to watch you skate because I thought it was your dream."

My bottom lip started to tremble. I couldn't speak.

"I will get some details about the girls' hockey program," he said. "Then we will see about next season."

"Do you mean it, Dad?"

He stood and wrapped his big arms around me. "Sí."

Looking up into his deep brown eyes, I found the courage to ask, "Do you think Mom would understand? She always thought I would be a champion skater."

He gave me a little squeeze. "She would want you to be happy. It's what we both want."

"If I could only talk to her ..."

There was a long silence. Then Dad whispered, "Talk to her from your heart. She will listen."

"Dad, I've tried, over and over. I never get an answer."

4 Falling Hard

September is usually a double disappointment — first I have to give up summer, and then I get dragged back to school. But I had to admit, so far, grade seven had been pretty amazing. My teacher, Mr Pullen, was cool — for an old man. Yin, Brooke and Amanda were in my class and we were all looking forward to playing hockey. Best of all: Todd Marshall had been living in British Columbia since June while his father was on a work assignment. I didn't know when he was coming back, and I didn't care.

During the second week in September, my grandparents came to visit and bought me brand new hockey skates. They even insisted on paying for my hockey program. Gramps seemed especially excited. After all, he is a big hockey fan. You should have seen his face when he talked about his home team. "Hockey is number one in Thunder Bay," he boasted. "I'm at the arena every Friday night … haven't missed a game in fourteen years."

Gram took me aside to speak in private. "Before your mother died, she made me promise that you would be able to keep skating. Of course, she had meant figure skating. But dreams change and she would understand."

I wish I could be sure.

By the end of September I was at the community centre arena for the team selections. Unlike rep hockey where players must try out to make the team, everyone who signs up to play house league automatically gets on a team. Even so, there would be group of coaches watching closely to assess each girl's hockey skills so that the teams they put together would be even and competitive.

I picked up my hockey skates and ran my fingers over the smooth blades, inhaling the scent of the new leather. Then, just like Cinderella, I slipped them on — a perfect fit — and began to lace up. There was another scent, one I tried to ignore: the lingering odour of old hockey sweat, even after I had baked the pads in the sun for three days.

When I left the dressing room, the Zamboni was flooding the ice, leaving the surface as smooth as glass. Waiting by the gate, I felt a shiver of excitement. It had been five months since I had been on skates, and I missed the thrill of the ice.

The community centre arena was not fancy. There

were two sets of bleachers: one for the home team fans and one for the visitors. There was a snack bar that advertised cheese nachos, giant pretzels, hot dogs and hot-buttered popcorn. So-o-o good — only it was hardly ever open.

Once the Zamboni had made its exit, I stepped onto the ice. "Whoa!" I clutched my stick, feeling wobbly.

Yin skated over to me, wearing a yellow practice jersey. "We're supposed to warm up by skating around the rink a few times," she said and headed off. "Come on, let's go."

Anxious to catch up, I pushed off with my right foot. All of a sudden, I lost my balance and went flying forward, landing on the ice. "Huh?" I looked around for an explanation.

Yin came gliding back. "Did someone push you?"

"I don't know," I replied honestly. "But this padding sure works." I stood up, feeling silly.

"Come on," Yin said, skating backwards.

I pushed off again and fell on my face.

Yin's mouth fell open. "Maya, what's wrong?"

"The skates," I groaned. I picked myself up again. Cautiously, I took a few baby steps, then a small push ... Whomp! Down again. My stick shot across the ice, tripping another girl.

I glanced over at some coaches who were observing me. How could this be? Maya Sanchez, top figure skater, turning into a jellyfish. Baby-stepping to the boards, I grabbed onto the ledge with my free hand. A girl in a Maple Leafs jersey skated over and handed me my stick.

"Hey, Maya."

"Jess!" I exclaimed, recognizing an old friend from figure skating. "You play hockey?"

She rapped her knuckles on my helmet. "Duh ... for two years." Pointing at my feet, she said, "Hockey skates don't have toe picks or heels. That's why you can't skate."

"What! No one told me." Then I remembered running my finger over the smooth blade of my hockey skates. I should have known.

"Same thing happened to me," Jess said. "You'll be okay, once you find your balance. Just don't try any fancy jumps in hockey skates. You'll land on your butt every time."

Jess skated off to join the crowd of girls who were gathering by the goal line. Nearby, I saw a long, red ponytail hanging out from a helmet, and I knew it had to be Amanda. She had stopped skating and was speaking to another girl.

"Amanda," I called. "Come here."

"You come here," she said, not moving.

"I can't skate!" I cried.

That got her attention. "What do you mean?" she said, gliding over.

"I have to learn all over," I said, "without using heels and toe picks."

"Well, you'll have to learn fast," she replied. "The drills are about to begin."

"Drills?" My knees went weak. "This sounds like torture."

Amanda wasn't listening. She skated off to join the other girls.

A gruelling hour later, I stumbled off the ice. In the dressing room Brooke put a hand on my shoulder. "Don't worry. You'll get used to it. Eventually."

I shot her a dirty look. "Thanks."

* * *

It had been a whole week since the team selections and I still hadn't received a phone call from my new coach. Ever since my disaster on ice, I had been freaking out, worrying that no coach would want me. But eventually the call came.

"Hello, Maya," a cheery voice said. "This is your hockey coach calling. My name is Mrs Duval."

My heart leaped into my throat. There was so much I wanted to ask, but all I managed to say was, "Hi."

"I understand this is your first year playing hockey," she said, "and that you had a little trouble on the ice the other day. Don't worry, house league hockey is all about learning and having fun."

"Okay."

"Our first practice is at six this Wednesday morning. Now," she went on, "I have a bit of homework for you. Our team has been assigned grey jerseys. I am asking each player to think up a good name for our team. At the first practice, we will vote on a name."

"Okay," I said, still short of words. Guess you could say I was overwhelmed.

The next morning the bus was overloaded by the time it pulled up to my stop. I had to sit in the front seat, beside some little kid who was already chowing down on his lunch — a bologna sandwich oozing with mustard. I watched in amazement as the mustard seeped through the holes in the bread. "You're not supposed to eat on the bus," I noted.

The boy smiled, showing me a row of slimy yellow teeth. He took another bite and the mustard squirted out of the sandwich. "Hey, look out!" I said, backing away. "That stains."

When the bus arrived at the school, Yin, Brooke and Amanda raced up to me.

"What team are you on?" Yin asked, grabbing my arm.

Crossing my fingers, I said, "Grey."

Brooke and Yin started cheering and giving me high-fives.

"We are all on the same team!" Brooke exclaimed.

Amanda was the only one who didn't look happy. "The new coach seems weird," she complained. "Last night, she called and said, 'Amanda, I hear you are a good stickhandler. You should be able to dribble the puck right past the other team.'"

"Dribble?" Yin said, making a face. "Right idea. Wrong sport."

As usual, Brooke was informed of the situation. "Mrs Duval is a drama teacher at the high school," she explained. "My sister says she has never played hockey. Truth is, she can hardly skate."

Amanda kicked the ground. "Ah, man! Just my luck! When my dad finds out, he'll probably try to switch me to another team. Like, how can she coach hockey if she has never played?"

Amanda had a good point. Natasha had been a competitive skater long before she became a coach.

"The league was short of volunteers," Brooke explained. "The hockey convener begged Mrs Duval to coach, and she finally agreed … I guess cuz her daughter, Danielle, is on the team."

"How do you know all this?" I asked.

Brooke adjusted the bandana in her hair. "Jewel is in Mrs Duval's drama class. She's been begging Jewel to be our assistant coach."

Amanda stopped pounding her shoe into the dirt and looked up. "Now that would rock. Your sister — M.V.P. of the Linton Lasers would be coaching us!"

Brooke smiled. "Mrs Duval told Jewel that helping out the team would give her the community service credit she needs for high school. So my guess is …"

I broke away from the conversation. A new guy had stepped off the next bus. He was walking with Craig and Matt.

I elbowed Yin. "Who is that?"

Yin glanced over her shoulder and shrugged. "Beats me. He's probably in grade eight."

As he approached, I got a strange feeling. Something about him seemed familiar. "No way," I said to the girls. "It can't be …"

"It is," Amanda said, checking him out. "And he looks cute."

Something had happened to Todd over the summer. His hair wasn't glued to his head anymore; it shined and bounced as he walked. He wore grey cargo pants and a hooded sweatshirt — no stains! Plus, he had grown a lot taller.

As the guys walked past, Todd smiled at me and waved. I found myself waving back.

Amanda called out, "Hey Craig, did you get my e-mails? I sent you two last night."

He didn't answer.

Brooke squeezed my hand. "Did you see the way Todd looked at you?"

Amanda shot me a look. "That is so not fair. You don't even try, and Todd still likes you! I can't even get Craig to notice me."

I watched Todd run onto the field. "He seems so different."

"Different … how?" Brooke pressed.

I sensed a trap. "I don't know," I said, carefully choosing my words. "Just different."

Brooke pounced. "Aha! Just like I thought."

I dug my hands into my hips. "Just cuz Todd Marshall decided to wash his hair and change his clothes doesn't mean …"

She wasn't listening. "Looks like Todd had entered stage two. He's trying to dress and act cool, but trust me — he is still pretty clueless about girls." She threw her arms open. "This is amazing. It's just like the magazine says."

I stared at her in disbelief. "You still have that magazine?"

She smiled sheepishly. "I keep it in my night table … you know … as a reference guide."

This conversation was getting weird. I was actually relieved when the bell rang. Still, I couldn't help wondering whether or not Todd would be in my class. Not that it mattered. I was just curious.

O Canada played over the PA system, and no Todd. The morning announcements came and went; still no Todd. Mr Pullen instructed us to take out our science texts and read the section called "Flying without Wings."

A knock came on the door. I spun around in my desk as the principal poked her head in the door. "Excuse me, Mr Pullen. Your new student has arrived."

Todd walked into the room and took a seat near the back by the windows. Naturally, I had to see what was up with the "new" Todd, so I wandered over to the row of bookshelves behind his desk.

"So ..." I said, casually flipping through the pages of some book. "How was B.C.?"

Without looking up from his text, he mumbled, "Okay."

"See any whales?"

"We were inland."

Something was wrong. By this point, Todd should have launched an attack. And I should have been on guard, my hands prepared to deflect a paper airplane, an eraser or a spitball — whatever he threw my way. He was acting strange after his trip. He needed to lighten up. And I knew just the thing.

"Hey, Todd," I said, "what has sixteen legs, chatters like a chimpanzee and stings like a bee?"

He looked up and shrugged. "I give."

"Me too," I said, "but it's outside the window."

He turned quickly and saw nothing.

"Aha, made you look."

He shot me a 'not impressed' look. He was right — my joke wasn't funny. Who was acting like the moron now?

For some reason, he started to smile. "Hey, I've got one for you. What is the colour yellow, looks like it fell from your mouth and is grossing me out?"

I glanced around room. "I give."

"Me too," he said, "but it's on your shirt."

I looked down and saw a bright yellow mustard stain in the centre of my shirt. I tried to tell Todd, "It wasn't me. It was a kid with a leaky sandwich ..."

"Sure ... I believe you."

"Miss Sanchez ..." I spun around and saw Mr Pullen standing there. "Can you tell the class how helicopters and balloons are able to fly without wings?"

"Uh ... air power?"

"Nice guess," he said. "Now, get back to your desk and read."

Todd looked up and laughed. He finally found something funny. Me.

5 A New Kind of Game

Brooke's mom drove us to the first hockey practice. When we arrived at the arena, the dressing room was already filled with girls excitedly talking about the new season. Yin and I found a place together on the bench and began to get changed. As I was putting on my shoulder pads, the door flew open. In glided a woman wearing a royal blue cape. Her long black hair was twisted into a bun on the top of her head. Everyone stopped what they were doing and stared at the woman.

"She's wearing a puck on her head," Yin whispered.

"Sporty!" I commented.

"Hello, girls," the woman said, her smile sweeping across the room. "My name is Mrs Duval."

"I am excited to be coaching this season," she went on, "and even though I have never actually played hockey, I have been researching the game thoroughly in books. And I intend to be right out there with the team, every step of the way ... although, I admit I haven't worn my skates in fifteen years."

Several groans were heard around the room.

"Jewel Miller has agreed to be our assistant coach," Mrs Duval added. "She has kindly volunteered to help with skills' development. For those of you who don't know Jewel, she is captain of the Linton Lasers and plays centre for their starting line."

Amanda let out a loud, "Yahoo!"

"I have just enough time to dust off my skates before the practice," Mrs Duval said, heading to the door, "so I will meet you on the ice shortly."

Minutes before the team was scheduled to be on the ice, Jewel came running into the dressing room. I hadn't seen her since July. In that short time, she had gone through some significant changes. She used to have long brown hair down to her waist. Now it was cut short and she had added blonde streaks. Her nose was pierced with a tiny gold stud. One thing is for sure: that girl had perfected the locker room drill. In the time it took me to lace up my skates, she was fully dressed and out the door.

When I stepped onto the ice, I took a cautious glide and began skating slowly. After a few laps, something clicked. As long as I slowed down and concentrated on my turns and stops it felt good. Once I even attempted a simple bunny jump, but landed face first on the ice. Without toe picks, I was pretty much grounded.

Mrs Duval was limping by the boards when I skated over. "Are you okay?"

She smiled at me, but I could see the pain in her eyes. "I think my skates shrunk … or else my feet got fat. Either way, I can't feel my toes."

"You could wear your boots on the ice," I suggested.

"No," she said firmly. "I want to do this right." She blew the whistle and called out, "Everyone, line up at the goal line!"

Mrs Duval began the practice with power skating drills: skating the length of the rink full speed, stopping at the far end, and blasting back to the beginning. Jewel skated up and down the ice shouting, "Bend your knees, keep your heads up. Come on, girls, give it all you got!"

After everyone had completed this drill five times, we did the same thing again, only backwards. And after that, we skated crossovers around the face-off circles. Some of the girls had trouble crossing one foot over the other. My years of practice were finally starting to pay off, as I could skate circles around most of them. Now that I had found my balance, I was on my way to becoming a hockey player …

… Or not! Stickhandling drills were next. Jewel set up orange pylons down the length of the rink. I was supposed to weave the puck back and forth between the pylons. But each time my stick made contact with the puck, it shot off down the ice like a scared rat.

Jewel came skating over to me. "Hey, this isn't baseball."

"Huh?" I said, looking clueless.

"You're holding the stick like a bat," she explained. "You'll never be able to play that way."

Once she showed me the proper grip, I tried the pylon course again. But the puck still veered out of control.

After practice, Mrs Duval met the team in the dressing room. Somehow she managed to smile, even though she could hardly walk. It was obvious she had some juicy blisters.

"Good practice, girls," she said. "Nice to see everyone working hard. Now, before you leave, I would like to vote on a team name." She gazed around the room. "Any suggestions?"

Amanda got straight to the point. "Grey is boring."

"Yeah," another girl piped up. "Yellow is best. Can we switch colours, Mrs Duval?"

Everyone started shouting out their favourite colours.

Like a true teacher Mrs Duval raised her hand to silence us. "From now on," she said, "I would like everyone to call me Coach. And as for the team jerseys — they are quite striking. The grey is accented with white trim and bold black letters."

"Maybe we could call ourselves the Elephants," someone said in a mocking voice.

That got a good laugh, so another girl tried to top that one: "Rhinos!"

Coach's smile was fading fast.

Brooke helped turn things around. "How about Sharks?" she suggested.

"Cool," a couple of girls chorused.

"Eagles," I offered, and a few people cheered.

When there were no more suggestions, Coach said, "Let's take a vote between Sharks and Eagles."

The results were:

Sharks: 7

Eagles: 10

Eagles it was ... and everyone seemed pleased.

"One more thing," Coach said. "There is a shortage of goaltenders in the league. Unfortunately, our team didn't get a goalie. So, in order to be fair, I will rotate the position. Each week I will assign a different girl to play in net ... unless, of course, someone would like to volunteer."

No hands went up.

I nudged Yin. "I'm not taking a turn."

"I don't think we have a choice," she replied.

"That's what you think. I could never afford all that equipment."

Yin laughed. "Nice try. The Minor Hockey Association gives each team a set of goalie equipment."

Coach waved some papers in the air. "Don't forget to pick up a schedule. And I have some rules sheets for everyone to read. First game is Friday night at six o'clock."

Gulp! That was in two days, and I had never even scrimmaged!

The next day Amanda invited us to her house after school. Yin had piano lessons, so it was just Brooke and me. Amanda said we needed to talk strategy. Strategy! I barely knew how to play the game let alone worrying about devising fancy plans to win.

Amanda placed a bowl of ketchup chips in the middle of her kitchen table and poured each of us a glass of fruit punch. By this time, she had forgotten all about our strategy session. Now, the topic was boys.

"Don't you think Craig is cute?" she gushed.

"Nope," I said, crunching on a chip. "He smells like worms."

"Worms don't smell!"

"Yes, they do."

"Wanna bet?"

"Actually, I think the smell is his armpits," Brooke said.

"You're just jealous," Amanda said, "because Craig used to like you."

"So what?" Brooke said. "I didn't like him back."

Amanda ran out of the room and returned with a cordless phone. Tucking her long red hair behind her ear, she shot us a fruit punch smile — tropical pink and toothy. I watched as she dialled Craig's number by heart. With each unanswered ring, her fruity smile dropped a little further. Finally, she put the phone down and pouted. "No one's home."

"Craig has hockey practice after school," Brooke explained.

Amanda stiffened. "How do you know?"

Brooke smirked. "Cuz he told me."

"Oh yeah," Amanda said, "he told me too. I just forgot."

"Forget about Craig," I said, "I need help with the hockey rules."

Amanda took a sip of her punch. She looked annoyed that I had switched the topic. "Read the rule sheet," she said. "It's all there."

"I did … but I still don't understand off-sides."

She ignored me. "Hey, I have an idea." She picked up the phone and started to dial.

"Who are you phoning?" I asked.

She winked at me. "You'll see." Suddenly, her attention turned to the phone. "Hey, Todd," she said, in a syrupy voice. "What's up?"

"Amanda!" I whispered. "What are you doing?"

"Uh-huh … Maya is standing beside me right now. She wants to know if you like her."

I lunged across the table, trying to grab the phone from her hand, but she managed to duck under my arm. "Just a sec—" she paused, giggling. "I'll ask." She shot the phone behind her back. "Todd wants to know if you like him."

"Aaaaahhhhhh!" Running into the bathroom, I slammed the door behind me. Then I overheard Amanda add, "Sorry, Todd. Maya can't talk right now. She's going to the bathroom."

"Liar!" I cried, running into the hall.

"Okay. Bye," she said cheerfully, hanging up.

Brooke sat silently at the table.

I marched over to Amanda. "How could you?"

She gave an innocent shrug. "What did I do?"

"You told Todd I was going to the bathroom. That was so evil."

She tossed her hair over her shoulder. "It was just a joke. Don't get so mad."

"Well, it wasn't funny." I grabbed my jean jacket and headed for the door.

"Wait!" Amanda called. She looked surprised that I would actually leave. "Todd wasn't really on the phone. I was just pretending."

I let go of the door handle and faced her. "Why should I believe you?"

"Todd and Craig play on the same hockey team," Brooke offered. "They should both be at practice."

"Honest," Amanda said, "I wasn't talking to Todd.

I didn't think you would get upset. I'm sorry. Please don't go."

Clutching my jacket in both hands, I glared at her. "I'll stay … on one condition."

She looked sheepish. "Anything."

"Promise you will never phone Todd Marshall again."

"Promise," she said, crossing her heart.

She seemed sincere, so I dropped my jacket and returned to the table. We never did talk about hockey that day. Boys! They sure were making us act crazy lately — or as my dad would say: loco!

6 The Puck Is Dropped

Dad usually works at the Fiesta Mexican restaurant on Friday nights, preparing the weekly special: chicken enchiladas, rice and black bean soup. Somehow, this week, he got the night off to watch my first hockey game instead.

Before the game, I made macaroni and cheese, hoping my favourite food would chase away the butterflies in my stomach. But the macaroni tasted like cardboard, the cheese sauce was runny, and the butterflies remained.

On the way to the arena, Dad had a bad case of pre-game jitters. He couldn't sit still in the car. Every time he shifted his weight, the springs in the driver's seat creaked. "I want you to relax and have fun tonight," he said, speaking too fast. "Remember, Chiquita, hockey is just a game. Win or lose, it doesn't matter. You will be fine. Bueno!"

When I walked into the locker room, Coach was

handing out team jerseys. Her hockey puck hairdo was gone; instead her dark hair hung straight, touching her shoulders. I held my grey jersey out before me, reading the large black print: "Jerry's Roofing." On the back was the number 17. I smiled. Seventeen sounded like a lucky number.

As I got changed, I listened closely while Jewel called out the lines: "Amanda will play centre; Kristen, right wing, Maya, left wing; Yin and Courtney will make up the defensive line. On the next line, Tamara will play centre; Brooke, left wing ..." After I heard Brooke's name, I tuned out until I heard the word 'goaltender' followed by Danielle Duval's name.

From across the room, Danielle let out a loud groan. "My mother made me."

"Danielle is going to need everyone's support," Jewel said. "I am expecting a strong defensive effort."

Poor Danielle, she looked miserable, slumped in the corner under the big goalie pads. Too bad for her, being the coach's daughter.

Coach carried a large canvas bag into the room. Reaching inside, she brought out a magnificent eagle. Its head and tail were snowy white; its body covered in feathers of black, brown and grey. Two yellow eyes peered out over a beak that was hooked like a can opener.

Holding the eagle high above our heads, she said, "Since ancient times the eagle has been a symbol of courage and power."

"It's beautiful," Tamara said. "Did it used to be real?"

"No," Coach assured us, "simply a good imitation ... but nevertheless, a worthy mascot for our team." She perched the eagle on the bench. "Now," she said, "all we need is a cheer. Any ideas?"

Kristen called out, "I know a good one."

Coach's eyes lit up. "Super. Let's hear it."

She stood and chanted:

Beat 'em, bust 'em
That's the way,
Crush 'em, cream 'em
Make 'em pay.
Go-o-o-o Eagles!

"Oh, my," Coach said. "Enthusiastic ... but perhaps a tad harsh."

The dressing room was silent. Danielle hid her face in her hands, embarrassed by her mother.

"Any other suggestions?" Coach asked, gazing around the room.

No one responded.

Before the game, we joined the opposing team on the ice to warm-up. They wore green jerseys and called themselves the Gators. It wasn't my imagination — those girls were big. At the sound of the whistle, my team gathered on the home bench. Our mascot sat perched behind the glass, its eyes trained on the ice. I glanced over at Dad. This was it … there was no turning back. I was a hockey player.

As I skated to the face-off circle, my heart was pounding. I took my position opposite a green winger. No one spoke. The ref dropped the puck. Sticks clashed as Amanda wrestled the big green centre for the puck.

"Keep your eye on the puck, Amanda," her father yelled. "Fight for it!"

Yikes! Mr Neal sure had a loud voice.

Amanda poked the puck into the open. Kristen picked it up and started skating toward the Gators' zone. With a burst of speed, I raced across the blue line. The whistle blew.

"Off-side!" the ref called. He was pointing at me.

"Huh? What did I do?"

Yin skated over and quickly explained, "You can't cross the blue line before the puck."

"Oh. Wait … I still don't get it!"

Yin didn't hear. She was getting in position for the face-off. When the ref dropped the puck, the Gator centre took a swing and launched it at the boards. Another Gator came out of nowhere. She carried the puck across our blue line, all the way behind the goal; then, slipping around in front, she tucked the puck in our net — all this, before Danielle even knew what was happening.

When I returned to the bench, Coach put her hand on my shoulder. "You're doing great, Maya!" she said. "Keep up the good work."

I hadn't played well, but it was still nice to hear some encouraging words. After my first shift, I realized the action on the ice is faster than it looks from the bench. When I was out there, my eyes were darting back and forth, the puck was zipping here and there, and I was skating in circles.

To start the next shift, Amanda won the face-off. The puck slid in my direction. Racing toward it, I drew my arms back, took a hard swing ... and missed. The puck slipped between my skates, where a Gator picked it up and passed it to her teammate. Yin chased after her and stole the puck. Meanwhile, another Gator was closing in fast. I skated over to help.

"Maya, get back!" Jewel called. "Play your position!"

Yin flipped the puck to Amanda who guided it smoothly past the Gators' defense. The puck fastened like a magnet to her stick. As she closed in on the goal, she brought her stick back over her head.

"Bend your front knee!" Mr Neal instructed from the bleachers. "Keep a tight grip on that stick ..."

Amanda hesitated for a moment, then ... Wham! She followed through with a hard slap shot. The puck hurtled up and over the boards."

"Aw, nuts!" Mr Neal yelled. "Amanda, work on your timing!"

Back on the bench, I guzzled some water and followed the action on the ice. A Gator carried the puck into our zone. Brooke was in hot pursuit, skating alongside her. Before Brooke could knock the puck away, the girl shot at the net. Danielle got caught up in her goalie pads and fell as the puck slid by her into the net. Score 2-0: Gators.

Before I knew it, my line was back on the ice. Amanda shot the puck to the boards. Courtney scrambled to get the loose puck and fired it back to Amanda who was wide open. Amanda stickhandled the puck up the ice, dodging every green jersey as she approached the goal.

"Go for the wrist shot!" Mr Neal called. "Shoot! Now! What are you waiting for?"

I glanced up and noticed his face was a strange shade of purple.

Amanda closed in on the net. She wound up and sent the puck sailing smack into the goal post. A perfect miss!

By the end of the game, the score was 5-0 for the Gators. Even though I had hardly touched the puck, I still managed to get three off-side violations. It wasn't an easy rule to learn.

In the dressing room, Coach did her best to cheer up the team. "Don't worry about the score," she said. "An eagle's first flight often ends in a crash landing. The important thing is that we pick ourselves up and get ready for the next game. I just know that someday this team will soar."

By the looks on the players' faces, it was obvious no one was buying her pep talk.

Dad greeted me outside with a hearty "Bueno!"

"Dad," I said, dragging my equipment, "I was terrible."

He took my hockey bag, leaving me to carry the stick. "Don't be hard on yourself," he said. "First games are never easy."

On the way out of the community centre, I overheard two Gators talking. The first girl said, "Those Eagles were a joke. Their centre made a bunch of amazing misses and their goalie was a sieve."

"Yeah," the other girl said, "and what about the winger who kept getting called off-side. She didn't even know how to play!"

I stopped and glared at the girls.

"No importa," Dad said.

"Yes, it does matter," I fired back. "They can't talk about us that way!"

Dad placed a hand on my back, guiding me toward the exit. "Keep walking, Maya. Your team will get another chance to play the Gators."

During the car ride home, Dad and I were both quiet. The radio helped to fill the silence.

7 Titanium Nerves

I had to hand it to Mrs Duval. She was giving the coaching job her best shot. At the next practice she brought along a Junior A goalie named Brett Holloway to give the team some goaltending instruction. As well, she had purchased second-hand hockey skates and a pair of gloves. At least now she looked like a hockey coach.

To start the practice, Coach divided us into two groups. Brooke and I got sent to the far end of the rink for Brett's goaltending clinic. He met us in full gear. His mask was like a piece of art work designed to ward off evil spirits. It was black with a set of long, white teeth along the jaw line. Near the top, a pair of red eyes kept lookout.

"Stand back," he cautioned us. Raising his large glove, he gave Jewel a signal. In response, she came sweeping down the ice and took a hard shot. The puck went high to the upper corner of the net. Brett reached out and caught it in his glove. Jewel picked up another puck and skated in a wide loop before firing a wrist shot. Falling to his knees, Brett made a lightning fast body save. Jewel took a few more tricky shots on goal, and Brett stopped every one.

When Jewel returned to the other end of the rink, Brett removed his mask. A mop of dark hair spilled out.

"Wow," Brooke gushed. "You are awesome! I mean … as a goalie."

He smoothed back his long hair and smiled, revealing a perfect set of teeth.

Brooke sighed out loud.

"Get a grip," I told her.

Leaning against the net, Brett began to speak. "The goalie has the most difficult job in hockey," he said. "Guarding the net takes a special kind of player. One who has a good eye, quick reflexes and nerves of titanium."

"Titanium?" Tamara said. "What's that?"

"A metal stronger than steel."

I frowned at Brooke. "Count me out. My nerves are made of itchy bumps. It would be a nightmare to get a rash under that heavy equipment."

"Before we begin," Brett said, "let me demonstrate some stretches."

"Stretches!" Courtney groaned. "I thought we were here for goalie instruction — not gymnastics."

"The goalie is a type of gymnast," he said. "She must stretch before each game or risk injury when she dives for the puck or slides to protect the corners of the net."

Brett went through a series of simple stretches. Then, without any effort, he dropped into the splits. When I did the same, he looked surprised; it was like he had never seen anyone else do the splits. As for the rest of the group, they wouldn't even try.

Next Brett taught us the goalie stance. We had to bend our knees and stick out our butts. "Better get comfortable," he said, grinning. "A goalie needs to hold that position for much of the game."

At first it was easy to hold the stance, but after a few minutes, my thighs started to burn, and then I got a butt cramp. "Yeow!" I cried, jumping up.

Brett laughed. "It just takes practice." He skated in front of the net. "Okay, now I'm going to show you how to make saves."

"About time," Brooke said, patting her sore butt. "This should be easier."

"Okay," he said. "Let's say someone takes a shot on net. In a split second the goalie must choose the best save to stop that puck."

"Yikes!" Brooke cried, backing up. "Take me home."

Brett demonstrated how to use the blocker and make glove saves. The big gloves felt awkward and we didn't get much time to practice, but at least we got the idea. Next he showed us how to use the goalie stick to block shots. But he kept the best moves for last — the body saves. Hurling one's self in front of a speeding puck couldn't help but be fun. When it was my turn in net, I dropped down on my knees, swinging my legs out at right angles as Brett instructed, and actually stopped a puck.

"Nice reflexes!" Brett said. "A perfect butterfly."

A compliment — from an older, very cute, Junior A goalie. I blushed and was glad to be wearing a helmet.

When I got back in line, Brett skated over to me. "How come you're so flexible?"

I shrugged. "Figure skating, I guess."

"You'd make a good goalie," he said. "You are a natural."

I didn't feel like telling him about my urticaria. That would not be cool.

Brett skated over to speak to the coach, then circled back.

"Oh wow," Brooke said, bubbling over. "I didn't think that goalies could sk—" She hesitated.

"Skate," he said, finishing her sentence. "Most goalies are excellent skaters. Goalies are usually the best skaters on the team."

"No way," Tamara piped up. "Centre rules!"

"Wingers! Wingers!" Brooke chanted, and I joined in.

"Defense!" Courtney yelled. "We save your butts."

Brett just laughed. "Okay, girls, listen up: You've learned a few basic moves today — enough to help in your next game. When your turn to play in net comes up, go out there and have fun."

I would have preferred to stay with Brett for the whole practice, but it was time to move to the stick-handling drills. As I skated to the other end of the rink, Amanda glided up to me. "Guess who's watching?"

My eyes scanned the boards and eventually came to rest on Todd and Craig.

"Think they're waiting for us?" she asked.

I shook my head. "They're probably waiting for a ride."

"Come on." She nudged me. "Let's find out."

"No way!"

"Party pooper," she sang out. "I'll go by myself."

While Amanda went to talk to the guys, I skated over to Coach. She was in bad shape — hanging onto the boards to stand up.

"It will get better," I assured her. "Same thing happened to me when I switched from white to black skates. You just need practice."

She grimaced. "No one told me it was going to be this difficult."

"I know exactly what you mean," I said, making an evil face at the orange pylons set out on the ice. Skating into the line-up, I gripped my stick and narrowed my eyes at the puck by my feet. "You better behave today," I warned.

At the sound of the whistle I took off, preparing to weave in and out of the pylons, controlling the puck all the way. But as usual, the puck took off, sliding across the ice. I sped after it yelling, "You dirty rat. Get back here!"

Jewel spun around on her skates, laughing. "Hey, it's just a piece of rubber. But whatever works for you."

I looked over at Todd. His nose was pressed against the glass. Oh, no! He had watched me spaz out! Calling the puck evil names, I skated to the back of the line.

After practice, as the team filed off the ice, my eyes surveyed the arena. Todd was nowhere in sight. For some reason, I got changed faster than the other girls, so I grabbed my hockey bag and headed out. Trying to juggle my bag and stick, I fumbled with the door handle, until I finally pulled it open and stumbled through.

"Ow-w-w!" came a cry from the other side.

I had accidentally hit Todd in the nose with the butt-end of my stick.

"I'm so sorry."

He was bent over, holding his nose.

I started to worry. "Are you okay?"

He looked up. His eyes were drawn back in pain. When he removed his hand from his nose, a red river rushed down his face.

"Oh no!" I cried. "This isn't good." Scrambling through my hockey bag, I found a white towel — the same one I used to dry my skate blades.

He held the towel over his nose and breathed out of his mouth. "I'm okay," he said, when he was able to talk. "It's nothing."

"Does it hurt?"

"Actually, I can't feel a thing. My nose is numb."

Just then, Amanda, Yin and Brooke burst though the heavy doors.

"There you are," Yin said. "We were ..." Upon seeing Todd, she forgot what she was saying.

Brooke dropped her equipment and stared. "Whoa, what happened to you?"

Todd removed the blood-soaked towel. His nose looked bigger than usual, but at least the bleeding had stopped. "A high stick," he said, with a straight face.

"But you looked okay after your game," Brooke said, looking puzzled.

Todd didn't answer. He just grinned my way.

"Where's Craig?" Amanda asked, looking hopeful.

"Gone home," Todd replied.

Her face dropped and she looked away.

Brooke nudged Yin, and they gave each other a knowing look. "We'll be waiting at the entrance," she said, dragging Amanda along with them.

"We'll let you know when my mom arrives," Yin called.

Todd and I were alone again. He leaned against a wall and stared at some little kids who were chasing each other. Neither of us could think of anything to say. An awkward moment. Finally, I blurted out the first thing that popped into my head. "How come you're still here?"

"I — uh — missed my ride," he stammered. "After my game, I stopped to watch ... Brett Holloway." Another awkward moment. Then he touched his nose and smiled. "Hey, I got the feeling back."

"And you're not looking like a ghost anymore," I observed.

He laughed and seemed to relax. "So how'd your team get so lucky — getting help from Brett Holloway and Jewel Miller?"

"Coach is a high school teacher," I explained. "She has never played hockey, so she gets her students to help out. The goalie clinic was so cool."

"Brett bends like rubber," Todd said. "He can mould himself any which way to make a save. I saw him teach you the butterfly. You looked good."

"Thanks," I said. "I just wish the rest of the game were as easy. Sometimes, I think I should have stuck with figure skating."

"What did you expect?" he said. "You're learning. Your skating is awesome, but your shooting could use some help."

"Tell me about it!"

"If you want, you could practice on my driveway."

Did I hear correctly? Todd … asking me over? My face got all hot. "Yeah, that would be cool," I said, staring at the floor.

When I looked up, I noticed that Todd's face was the colour of a ripe tomato.

Another awkward moment.

Brooke came to the rescue, calling, "Maya, Yin's mom is here."

Before I could reply, Yin came running over. "Todd, do you need a ride? There's room in our van."

"Uh … sure," he said. "That would be great."

Before long, the van was loaded with people and hockey equipment. Todd and I ended up on the back bench crowded next to his hockey bag. Amanda grinned and said, "Oh, look, Maya and Todd are squeezed together like two lovebirds. Isn't that romantic?"

Todd stared out the window, twiddling his fingers on his lap. And I stared straight ahead. My whole life was turning into one big awkward moment.

8 Second Thoughts

Before the next game, Kristen came up with a cheer that Coach called very energetic. All we had to do was bang the butt-end of our sticks on the boards, a thunderous roar, and chant:

Hey, Hey (bang, bang),
Ho, Ho (bang, bang),
Hey (bang), Ho (bang),
Hey (bang), Let's Go!
Eagles R-R-R-OCK!! (more loud banging)

That night we were playing the Flames. The girls dressed in bright red jerseys. Not much was said in the Eagles' dressing room before the game started. Jewel gave us a few last-minute pointers, and then, after Coach's pep talk, we took to the ice.

They may have called themselves the Flames, but tonight the Eagles were hot. In the first minute of the game, Danielle fired a shot from just inside the blue line and scored. A goal by the defense! Her mother cheered loudly from the bench.

The chanting started. "Hey, Hey! (bang, bang) Ho! Ho! (bang, bang) …

Then Amanda got a beautiful breakaway. As usual, Mr Neal looked on grimly from the bleachers: "Stay low, keep your eye on the puck … move it, move it … dig in … come on, skate!"

Amanda took off as though she had been fired out of a rocket launcher. No one could catch her! She flew up to the net and flipped the puck, straight into the goalie's glove.

I glanced up at Mr Neal. His face was shades of red and purple. That man did not look healthy.

After that, Amanda seemed to lose her fire. And that signaled the beginning of the Eagle's meltdown. At the same time, the Flames were heating up. They went on to score two goals, one after another. Yin and Danielle played awesome defense, blocking shot after shot and clearing the puck. If they hadn't played so well, the score would have been a lot higher, especially considering what was happening in our net. Courtney was playing in goal, but she was afraid of the puck, so she ducked out of its way whenever it came near. Geez, you would have thought the Flames were hurling fireballs at her.

As for me, I made team history for getting the first

penalty of the season. We were in the second period, and trailing by one goal. A Flames player hit the puck, launching it into the air. I was standing right in its path. All I did was reach up with my glove and catch it. Then I threw it to Kristen. The whistle blew.

"Nice reflexes," Jewel called out. "But you're not a goalie."

The Eagles came back in the third period to tie the game. Tamara scored a beautiful goal with a wicked wrist shot. It was her first goal of the season, and she got so excited that she high-fived everyone — even one surprised Flames player. Our team was pumped — for awhile. The final score was 4-2 for the Flames.

* * *

After the awkward moment in Yin's van, Todd and I didn't speak to each other for a week. Finally one day when the class was doing research in the library, he walked up to me and said, "Hey, wanna see something?"

I watched with interest as he cupped his hands over his nose and mouth. Then, he pushed his nose to one side with his fingers, making a sickening crack.

My knees went weak. "Did I do that? Is your nose broken?"

"Want me to do it again?" he offered. "It doesn't hurt … much."

"No! That noise gives me the shivers."

Mr Pullen walked up behind Todd and tapped his shoe on the floor. "Mr Marshall," he said, "I think you owe Miss Sanchez an apology."

Todd whirled around to face the teacher. "Huh?" he said, shrugging innocently. "For what?"

"For pulling such an old prank. Even a guy like me has used it once or twice."

"Oh," he mumbled. "That."

I glared at Todd until he raised his hands as if he had just been arrested. "Okay … I give up."

"Show me!" I demanded.

"It's easy," he said, looking sheepish. "When you tweak your nose, just click your thumbnail on the back of a front tooth."

I cupped my hands over my face and produced such a loud crack that even Todd was shocked.

With that dumb joke, all the weird feelings between us vanished. It was the perfect ice breaker — or, should I say, nose breaker.

★ ★ ★

After school I phoned Taylor Wellington and asked if I could catch a ride to the Linton Heights Arena to watch the figure skating practice. Okay, I admit it — I missed figure skating, and I missed Natasha, and I missed being really good at a sport. Lately, I had been practicing my figure skating jumps on the living room rug, imagining my old routines in my head. I needed to talk to Natasha ... to see if she would take me back.

When we arrived at the arena, Taylor hurried to the dressing room, and I went to find Natasha. Her office door was closed, and when I knocked, there was no answer. Without warning, two strong arms grabbed me from behind, crushing me in a bear hug.

"There is my special girl," Natasha boomed. She released me long enough to spin me around to face her. Reaching out, she grabbed my cheek and gave it a yank. "How have you been, Maya Sanchez?"

"Good," I said. "Well, actually, just okay. Can I talk to you?"

"Of course." She unlocked the door to her office. "Come in. Tell Natasha all about it."

Natasha sat at her steel desk and directed me to the hard chair on the opposite side. Lacing her fingers together, she cracked her knuckles a few times. "Much better." She smiled with satisfaction. "Now, begin."

"I'm — uh — not sure if I did the right thing, leaving figure skating."

She leaned forward, placing her elbows on the desk. "Hockey ... is it not working out?"

"All I ever do is mess up."

"Hmmm," she said, studying my face, "have you given it your best shoe?"

"You mean, 'my best shot.'"

"Shoe … shot." She tossed a hand in the air. "Same thing."

"Yes, Natasha," I said, getting frustrated. "My very best shot."

She pounded her fist on the desk. "Good girl. Then go ahead, Maya … fail!"

Leaning my head in the palm of my hand, I sighed. "You mean succeed."

She pounded her fist again. "No. You must fail first. Fail, then try again … fail some more … just don't give up. Not until you know in your heart that hockey is not for you. Then I will welcome you back."

"But, Natasha!"

"You may not remember," she pressed on, "but when you first began figure skating, you kept dragging one leg behind you and falling. It took years of practice to become a good skater."

I dropped my head on the desk, wishing I hadn't come.

After a moment, she reached out and ruffled my hair. "Some people say I am not sensitive. But, Maya, I do care."

Just then my eyes started to water. I quickly wiped them with my coat sleeve.

"Maybe we can make a deal." She stood and walked over to me. "A business arrangement."

I sat up at attention.

"You come out to practice once a week and help

with the pre-school skaters. In return, I will make sure you get some ice time. That way if you decide to return to figure skating next year, you will be able to catch up to the others — quick as a beaver."

A smile crept onto my face. I didn't even bother correcting her. "Yes," I said, leaping off the chair.

She extended her hand out to me. "Is it a deal?"

I took her hand and shook it hard. "For sure," I said. "I just have to ask my dad."

"I would not have it any other way," she said.

We had already said goodbye when I ran back and hugged Natasha. She hugged me back, and I saw that her eyes were moist. Maybe Natasha wasn't sensitive on the outside, but she couldn't fool me — she was a cream puff on the inside.

After I left Natasha's office, I took a seat at the rink to watch the two top skaters. Taylor was wearing white leggings and a powder blue sweater. I watched as she aced the double Axel — the same jump that I had struggled to complete at the ice carnival. Kelly wore black warm-ups, and her hair was tied back into a long braid. She had just completed some intricate footwork and was winding down into a tight sit spin. A newspaper reporter stepped on the ice and tried to interview them, but Natasha promptly shooed him away. No one interrupts her figure skating practices. When skaters are on the ice, Natasha rules.

9 Private Moments

I got your note, Chiquita. What is this all about? You … figure skating again!"

I had just walked in the door and Dad was already on my case. I tried to dismiss him with a shrug. "It was nothing. I missed Natasha, and I wanted to say hi. That's all."

"Oh," he said, but there was a lingering question in his eyes.

"Oh, yeah … there is something else. Natasha asked if I could help her with the pre-school skaters."

Stroking his goatee, Dad searched my eyes, trying to read my mind. And he came awfully close. "Do you miss figure skating? Is that it?"

I wrapped a ringlet around my finger. "A bit," I admitted. "If I volunteer once a week, I can get some free ice time. And it won't interfere with my homework cuz I'll be home by five."

I thought he was going to have a major fit. Instead,

he just smiled and said, "Bueno."

I ran up to my bedroom to do some stretching. Natasha would never allow me to attempt any jumps if my body had lost its flexibility.

Later, I wandered down to the kitchen and found Dad wearing his white chef's apron. "Just in time," he said. "I am preparing tacos."

I watched him pull something green and prickly out of the fridge. It looked suspicious, so I asked, "What is that?"

"Fresh organic cactus." He took a knife and began filing off the prickles. "A lot of our customers are requesting vegetarian dishes, and they like exotic food. So tonight, I am experimenting — mixing black beans with slivers of cactus, then adding grated cheese, and smothering it all in sour cream and salsa. Sound good?"

"Dad, you're kidding, right? Black beans and cactus! I'd rather eat the plate."

"Just try it," he implored.

I folded my arms. "How do you know cactus is edible?"

"Not only is it edible," he said, "it tastes quite like green beans."

I watched as he filled the hard, corn flour shells. Then, with a few dramatic sweeps of his arms, he served up dinner.

He took a bite, then kissed his fingers. "Delicioso!"

"Can I make macaroni?" I asked.

He gave me his lovable lion look. "Oh, all right," I said. "One bite."

Holding my breath, I raised a taco to my mouth, and took a tiny bite, getting only shell and sour cream. "Not bad, Dad," I said, smiling. "I think your customers — the adults, that is — will love it. Now can I make macaroni?"

Before he could answer, I got up and was heading to the cupboard.

"Wait," he said, pulling me back. "I have something for you." He reached in his shirt pocket and brought out a necklace: a gold dolphin on a chain.

"It's beautiful," I said, reaching out to touch it. "Is it Bela?"

He nodded. "I bought this for your mother soon after we met."

I sat back down. "Tell me the story again."

"All right ... one more time." He smiled at me for a moment, and then his eyes drifted far away. "I had been up early that day cooking breakfast for the hotel guests. To escape the hot kitchen, I wandered down to the beach to visit Juan, the man in charge of the hotel's water sports. While we were talking, Juan noticed a woman in a small sailboat. She was waving her hands and calling for help. A large grey fin was circling her boat. Juan and I jumped into a motorboat and sped to her rescue. As we approached the sailboat, Juan slowed the engine, and I dove into the turquoise sea. After that, all the woman could see was rippling water. The fin and the man had disappeared. Suddenly, there came a big spray of water as I ripped through the surface like a bronze torpedo."

"Bronze torpedo! Dad, get real!"

"Shh! Let me tell the story ... The woman gasped as a huge creature rose up under me.

"'Buenos días, Señorita,' I said, flashing the pretty lady a smile. 'I am Felipe. And this is Bela.' I stroked the dolphin's smooth skin. 'We have been amigos for many years — ever since I was a young boy, fishing nearby with my father.'

"'Friends?' the woman said, leaning over the side to watch us. 'But this dolphin is wild.'

"'This dolphin has a good heart,' I told her.

"At that moment, the woman saw that I also had a good heart. And I knew I was looking into the eyes of an angel."

Dad stopped his story abruptly, and stared down at his taco. But I could tell he wasn't interested in food anymore.

"Dad," I said, breaking the silence, "if it hadn't been for Bela ... what I mean is, do you think she guided you to Mom that day?"

"Perhaps," he replied. "Ever since I was a boy, Bela looked out for me."

"Do you miss her?"

"Sí, I miss them both. Now … stand up and turn around."

I did as Dad said, and he fastened the necklace around my neck. Having Bela close to my heart felt good.

10 Parental Interference

On Sunday afternoon the Eagles were scheduled to play the Barracudas. Before the game Amanda called to say her father was sick with the flu, so Dad offered to drive her to the arena. When we picked her up, she was in a good mood, laughing and joking with me in the back of the car.

The Barracudas were tough, and the team had a couple of girls who played dirty. But in Sunday's game, it worked to our advantage, as they took three dumb penalties. For once, I was able to help my team. It was late in the first period. I was skating hard after the puck when a Barracuda slipped her stick between my skates, bringing me down. The whistle blew. The ref signalled 'tripping' and pointed to the offender. She got two minutes in the penalty box.

Thanks to me, the Eagles now had the advantage. Amanda lost the face-off, but I managed to intercept the puck and shoot it into the open. While the short-handed Barracudas were skating all over the ice trying to cover us, Amanda nabbed the puck and headed into their zone. As she crossed the blue line, her stick went back, and she followed through with a hard slap shot. The puck rose over the goalie's left shoulder, and right into the net.

Yin jumped on Amanda and they both fell down. The rest of us piled on top. Our best player was finally out of her scoring slump!

Kristen was playing in net that game — actually she was playing everywhere but in net. Whenever the puck came into our zone, she would get hyper and race out past the goal crease, leaving the net wide open. No one blamed Kristen. She had missed Brett's goaltending clinic, and it was obvious she was trying her best.

At the end of the game the score was tied 5-5. Amanda had scored three goals for a hat trick. Tamara and Brooke had scored one each. And I got the assist on Amanda's first goal. Yahoo! Everyone agreed we had outplayed the other team, and we vowed to win the next game. But for the time being, we were happy with a tie.

★ ★ ★

That evening Dad and I were in the kitchen washing dishes when the phone rang. Dad answered and immediately his eyebrows sprang up like two antennae. He hesitated before slowly passing me the receiver. "For you," he said. "It's a boy."

I snatched the receiver from his hand. "Hello."

"Hey, what's up?"

I recognized Todd's voice. "Nothin'," I said, keeping an eye on Dad.

"Oh. I — uh — just wanted to say that it's okay … you can come over tomorrow … that is if you want to … you know … practice shots."

My heart started to pound. "Just a minute. I'll ask." I called over to Dad. "Is it okay if I go to Todd Marshall's after school tomorrow to practice hockey?"

He put down the pot he was drying. "Isn't that the boy you call Toad — the one who annoys you?"

I pressed the receiver hard into my sweatshirt. "Dad! He will hear you!"

"Hmmm … you must have figure skating or hockey practice … or homework."

"No."

He looked bewildered.

"Dad," I said, measuring my words. "I-am-going-to-practice-hockey. That's all."

He shook his head indicating 'no.' But at the same time, his lips were saying, "Sí, you may go."

By then, my hands were in a sweat. The receiver slipped through my fingers and went crashing down on the tile floor. "Todd," I said, quickly recovering it.

"Are you still there?"

"Yeow … my ear! What happened?"

"Must be a bad connection."

"No problem," he said. "I'll switch ears. Hey, did your dad call you Chiquita?"

"No! He was talking to a banana. It's a … chef thing. They get really personal with food."

"Okay … Whatever."

"Anyway," I said, changing the subject, "I can come tomorrow, but I have to get off the phone now cuz, like, I have a ton of homework."

Actually, I didn't have any homework. The problem was Dad – he was listening to my every word. When I hung up, he dropped the dish towel and wandered to the living room.

"Dad," I said, following him. "I need to talk to you." I assumed a serious pose — arms folded, eyes narrowed. "It's like this," I began. "I don't want to be called Chiquita any more. I am too old. Besides, in Canada, Chiquita is a brand of banana."

He leaned forward in his chair. "But, Chiquita?"

"Dad …" I warned.

He tried his lovable lion look. This time, it didn't work. I wouldn't back down.

"When I lived in Mexico, my nickname was Chino," he said. "That means curly. All my Mexican friends had nicknames. Don't you see? Chiquita is my special name for you."

"Dad," I said, holding my ground. "Right now, I just want to be called Maya."

"Ay, ay, ay!" He threw his hands up. "Maya it is."

I hugged him hard. "Thanks, Dad."

★ ★ ★

On Monday morning, it was school as usual … that is, until Amanda vanished during morning recess. Brooke was worried about her strange disappearance.

"I sat with Amanda on the bus this morning," she told Yin and me. "She hardly said a word; she just stared out the window."

"That's not like Amanda,"Yin said, her eyes widening. "She hardly ever stops talking — especially about Craig."

We each agreed to search a different section of the schoolyard and not give up until one of us found her. After I had checked out the girls' washrooms, I wandered around to the narrow patch of gravel that is usually deserted at recess. There I found her, leaning against the wire fence that separates the yard from the parking lot. Her head was downcast. She didn't notice me walk up and when I called out, "Hey, Amanda, great game on Sunday!" she didn't even smile.

"I can't wait to play the Rockets this Friday night," I went on. "Now that your game is back on, I bet we will blast them to Mars."

Amanda looked at me with a blank expression. "You don't get it," she muttered.

"Get what?" I said. "Hey, I can only dream of getting a hat trick."

She kicked a stone, sending it flying through the air.

"Amanda, what's wrong?"

She didn't answer. So I just stood there, staring her down, until she finally cracked. "Didn't you notice how quiet the arena was last night?"

"Yeah, now that you mention it ... your dad wasn't there. He is kind of loud."

"Loud! He totally psyches me out."

"Well, maybe if you explain to him—"

"I've tried. He doesn't listen. He actually thinks he's helping me. Ever since he and Mom got divorced, he tries too hard at being a good dad. You know what? He needs to get a life of his own."

"So," I said, "let me get this straight. If your dad is at the game, you can't score."

She booted a stone at the sun. "Bingo!"

"Whoa, that stinks!" Joining her at the fence, we both slumped over. All of a sudden, an idea sparked in my brain. "Maybe I can help."

"What? Kidnap Dad before each game?" She let out a weak laugh.

"I've got to talk to someone first," I said. "Then I'll get back to you," I said, and convinced Amanda to join the others.

As we walked around the corner of the school, Amanda's face suddenly lit up: "Hey, there's Craig!" she exclaimed. And she just took off like I didn't exist.

At the end of the day, Yin and I sat together on the bus. She was the only person I had told about my invitation to Todd's.

"So," she said, giggling. "Are you nervous?"

"Totally," I admitted. "What if I can't think of anything to say — or I say something stupid? Even worse, what if I break out in a rash?!"

"Just practice shots," she advised. "Then you won't have to talk."

I took a deep breath. "Good idea."

Yin leaned her head on my shoulder. "What about my problem?"

"You have a problem?"

"The game on Friday. I have to play in net. What if I let every shot in?"

"You'll do great," I assured her. But inside, I was really thinking that I would hate to be her.

When the bus stopped, I got off and walked three blocks to meet Todd. Then we walked to his house. As it ended up, I didn't have to worry about making conversation. He blabbed on about his last game, how he got two goals and an assist. Sounded like he was bragging … or trying to impress me.

When Todd's house came into sight, he had a fit. "What the—? No way!" The oak tree on his front lawn had shed a blanket of leaves all over the driveway.

"Wait here," Todd said. He disappeared into his garage, and a few minutes later came out carrying a rake.

I started to laugh. "What are you going to do — rake the driveway?"

"No, you are."

At that, he turned and walked into his house, leaving me holding the rake.

What a jerk! I thought, kicking a bunch of leaves. How could I have been so stupid to think he had changed? He was still the same old Toad.

I threw the rake on the driveway, stomped over to the oak tree, and grabbed my backpack. Upon hearing the front door open, I glanced back. Todd approached with a broom in his hand.

"Hey," he shouted. "Where are you going?"

Reaching into my backpack, I brought out a pack of gum. "Want one?"

Once Todd and I had cleared the leaves off the driveway, he brought out his net, along with a couple of sticks and a bucket of pucks. I watched as he flipped a few pucks in the top corners of the net, making it look easy. Then he turned to me. "What do you want to practice? Your wrist shot … or maybe, I could shoot you some passes, and you could practice tipping the puck into the net."

"How about the slap shot," I suggested.

He glanced at the window in his garage. "That shot is hard to control."

"But it looks so cool!"

He shrugged. "Oh, what the heck."

"One more thing," I said, "I haven't learned it yet."

Todd's face went white, but he made a fast recovery. "No problem," he said. "I'll show you how."

He demonstrated the high back swing and the fast follow through. It looked pretty easy, so I stepped up to the puck. "Stand back," I warned. "Here goes nothing!"

Raising the stick high behind me, I wound down hard, making solid contact with the puck. Whomp!

Todd hit the ground and started rolling. "Owww ... my shin!"

Dropping the stick, I ran over to him. "Are you okay? Do you need ice?"

He managed to hop up on one leg. "I'll be okay," he said, "soon as I can put my foot down."

"Guess my aim stinks, eh?"

He looked at me, and for an instant, I thought I saw fear in his eyes. "You sure hit hard."

"Hey, I have an idea," I said. "When you are able to walk, maybe you could show me the tip in."

"Sure." He grimaced. "It's safer."

An hour later, when I left for home, I was feeling pretty confident about the next game. When I walked in the door, the phone was ringing.

"What's up?" Amanda asked, when I answered.

"Nothin'," I replied.

"That's not what I heard … you were over at Todd's."

"Yeah … so?" My mind started to race. How did Amanda know?

"I can't believe you hit him," she said, working herself into a fit of laughter.

"How do you know?" I demanded.

"Todd told me. That … and more."

"B-but that's impossible. I just got in the door. Wait a minute … did you phone him?"

"Of course not, I wouldn't break our promise. If you must know, I was chatting with Todd on the Internet."

"Same thing!" I roared.

"No, it's not," she said, sounding hurt. "Anyway, that's not why I phoned. You promised you'd get back to me, you know, about my dad."

I clenched my jaw, trying hard not to explode. "I just got home. I haven't even …"

"Okay, okay, I'll talk to you when you're in a better mood."

To be honest, I wasn't sure I wanted to help Amanda anymore.

After I hung up the phone, I stared into space, trying to figure things out. What was with Amanda? Was she even my friend anymore? And if so, why was she acting sweet one minute and then mean the next?

11 Message from Mom

Surprise!"

Gram came running down the driveway with Gramps shuffling along behind. It was Friday afternoon and I had just stepped off the school bus. Swinging my backpack off my shoulders, I ran to greet them.

Gram doesn't look like a grandmother. She dyes her grey hair light brown and wears bright colours. That day she was dressed in navy pants and a red sweater with little white buttons shaped like anchors. On the other hand, Gramps does look like a grandfather. His head is bald except for a thin line of grey hair fringing his ears. He wears baggy grey pants and suspenders.

After Gram smothered me in a hug, Gramps reached out and tweaked my ear. "We've come to watch your game."

"But it's Friday," I said. "The Thunder Bay team is playing. And you haven't missed a game in … how long?"

"Fourteen years," he said. "Until now, I haven't had a better offer."

My eyes bugged out. "No way!"

He ruffled my hair. "I just wish we could be here for more of your games."

Gram took my hand. "Come here, sweetheart, I have something to show you."

I followed her to the living room where she unzipped her overnight bag and brought out some papers that had yellowed with age.

"Your grandfather found these in the attic," she said, handling them with particular care.

By the way Gram was acting, I could tell the papers were important. I searched her face for a clue. Her eyes were moist and her mouth was quivering. All of a sudden, I felt afraid.

She handed me the papers and said, "It's a speech that your mother wrote when she was in grade seven. I think she would like you to have it now."

I glanced down and read the title: My Olympic Dream. A lump rose in my throat. I couldn't speak.

Gram nudged Gramps. "Come along, Joe, you need to stretch your legs after the long drive."

Gram handed him his coat. "We'll be back in a few minutes, darling," she called, as she pushed Gramps out the door.

Alone in the house, I stared down at the page and began to read:

> Gliding onto the ice, I struck my pose. At the sound of the music, my arms unfolded, my skates jolted into jazzy dance steps, and then I took off in a burst of speed, completing a combination of jumps … A successful routine would bring me one step closer to my dream …
>
> Mrs Smith and classmates: My dream is to represent Canada in the Olympics …

As I read my mother's words, I felt as if she were in the room with me. If I kept reading, maybe, just maybe, I could keep her close:

> During the opening bars of my music, I become a china figurine, still and perfectly posed, while inside I am crumbling with fear.

My eyes wandered from the page. Mom had never told me she got competition jitters. She had always seemed so confident.

I read on, hungrily devouring each word:

> … One day, I saw an ad in a skating magazine for a product called Magic Hair Varnish. It was guaranteed to make a skater's hair shine and to hold it in place throughout the most demanding performance. Knowing that my father kept

> an aerosol can of varnish in the basement, I asked my friend Emily to spray my hair before a provincial competition. Wow, did it ever shine! In fact, my hair looked and felt like polished oak. That's when I knew something was wrong. So I ran to wash my hair. No luck. The varnish was permanent. When my mother saw me she let out a shriek, then grabbed her purse and rushed me to the hairdresser who cut off my long hair.

I smiled to myself. So that's why Mom wore her hair so short.

I didn't want to reach the end, for at that moment, everything felt right — Mom and I were together and she was sharing her stories, making me cry and making me laugh — helping me to know her ... to remember. But the end did come, and I was left alone again. But to my surprise, I was smiling. For with her parting words, Mom left behind a gift. She had written: "Every girl should follow a dream — a dream of her own."

There it was — the answer. Mom had found a way to reach me. I read the same words over and over — until I believed them in my heart. Hot tears flowed down my cheeks. Good tears. Mom would want me to have a dream of my own.

Mom never did make the Olympics. She fell and broke her ankle in practice. But she was still a champion.

★ ★ ★

That night Dad was working at the Fiesta, so Gram and Gramps drove me to the arena. After I found them a good spot on the middle bleacher, I hurried to the dressing room. As I pushed open the door, Amanda came running up to me.

"Okay, let's go over the plan," she said, grabbing my arm. "Your old figure skating coach is coming to the game. And she is going to fix things with my dad. How, exactly?"

"It's like I told you," I said. "Natasha does not like parents interfering with the coaches or players. She is a convincing woman. I get the feeling she will take care of your dad."

"A feeling is not a plan," Amanda said. "And what do you mean 'take care of my dad?'"

I didn't answer her because Coach had just arrived to give the team a pep talk. I joined Yin on the bench. Yin is not big in the first place, and the goalie gear swallowed her up.

"I hear the Rockets are tough to beat," I said, as I reached in my bag.

Yin bent over on the bench. "I feel sick. I have to go to the washroom."

"You can't. You're wearing too much equipment."

She didn't reply. She was too busy removing the pads. I watched helplessly as she sprinted to the washroom. I had no choice but to let her go alone cuz hearing other people get sick makes me sick. Then the team would be short two players.

A few minutes later, Yin walked out of the washroom looking pale.

"Are you okay?" I asked.

She nodded. "I think it was something I ate for dinner."

"Chicken?" I asked. Then I added two flapping arms. "Bawk! Bawk!"

She didn't think my joke was funny. "Just wait, Maya. Your turn is coming."

Gulp! She had to remind me.

The Rockets looked confident in their navy blue jerseys. As I warmed up on the ice, I spotted Natasha sitting on the middle bleacher next to Gram and Gramps. Mr Neal had taken his usual place on the top bleacher where his voice boomed over the glass.

As the ref was about to drop the puck, Mr Neal was testing out his lungs: "Get down low, Amanda! Dig for the puck!"

Glancing over my shoulder, I saw Natasha's head swivel in Mr Neal's direction.

Things were going as planned.

The ref dropped the puck. With a flick of her wrist, Amanda shot the puck out of the face-off circle. Kristen picked it up and skated into the Rocket's zone.

"Use your brain, Amanda!" Mr Neal hollered. "Get

out in the open! Watch your form! You're leaning too far forward!"

Natasha rose from her seat and walked up to Mr Neal. I got the feeling the action on the bleachers was going to be hotter than anything on the ice.

Kristen made a clean pass to Amanda. Dodging a line of blue jerseys, Amanda skated close to the goal line. She flipped the puck up over the goalie and straight over the net, after which she came rushing at me, yelling, "Thanks for nothing!"

Meanwhile, up in the bleachers, Natasha and Mr Neal were talking, and by the looks on their faces, they were having an intense conversation. I tried to read their lips, but it was impossible, for I was too far away.

When I returned my attention to the game, the Rockets were rushing toward our net. Yin stood in the goalie stance. Unfortunately, she froze in that position — didn't move a muscle as the black missile was launched past her elbow. All I can say is she made one fine ice sculpture.

"That's okay, Yin," I called. "You'll get it next time."

When my line returned to the ice, the Rockets won the face-off. Their winger skated with the puck into our zone. Courtney intercepted and shot the puck down the ice. I skated hard, picking it up and shooting it over to Amanda. She got into position and slammed a beautiful wrist shot into the net. The crowd stood and cheered. Amanda just stood there looking stunned. Suddenly she burst into a fast skate and threw herself on the ice. It was a victory slide all the way to the blue line!

Amanda scored again in the next period. When we were sitting together on the bench, she leaned over and said, "I have no idea how you did it … but thanks."

I glanced up at Mr Neal and Natasha. They were laughing. Huh? That wasn't part of my plan. In fact, it was downright odd.

Near the end of the third period, the score was tied 4-4. Amanda had scored her second hat trick of the season, and Kristen had also put one away. Yin had finally thawed out in net and made a couple of difficult saves.

Both teams were tense. With one minute left things didn't look good for the Eagles. The Rockets had control of the puck, and they were closing in on our net. Yin stood ready. The missile went zooming toward the goal. Reaching out with her glove, Yin made the save.

Thirty-eight seconds: Amanda kicked the puck ahead with her skate to win the face-off. Kristen scrambled after the loose puck. At the same time, Rockets were being launched all around her. She panicked and took a wild shot. A Rocket picked up the stray puck and sped out of the zone. Meanwhile, Amanda was in hot pursuit. Sneaking up behind the girl, she poked the puck away to Kristen who began stickhandling up the ice.

Sixteen seconds: Amanda positioned herself in front of the goal. Kristen came up the right side. Amanda banged her stick on the ice. "I'm open!" she cried.

Kristen slammed a shot right through a pair of blue socks. Amanda nabbed the puck and drove it at the net. The goalie dove and made the save.

Rebound!

Six … five … four …

Amanda threw herself on the ice, knocking the puck forward with her stick. It slowly dribbled through the crease to the left of the net where I was standing. Positioning my stick, I tipped the puck. The crowd went wild as the buzzer signalled the end of the game. Score 5-4: Eagles.

My whole team came swooping down, flattening me on the ice. Coach congratulated me for scoring the winning goal and handed me the puck. "A souvenir of your first goal," she said.

I gripped the puck in my hand as though it were a gold medal.

12 Smooch ... Smooch

Jewel walked up to me as I was loosening my skates. "Nice going!" she said. "You played like Hayley Wickenheiser tonight. Where'd you learn that fancy tip-in?"

"A friend," I said, yanking my foot out of my skate.

"Her boyfriend," Amanda sang out from across the room. "Todd Marshall."

I shot Amanda a dirty look, but that didn't slow her down. "They've been making some hot moves on his driveway," she added.

By now the whole locker room was listening. I pulled off my other skate, then stood and marched over to Amanda.

"What are you talking about?" I said, aiming a finger at her. "You weren't even there. For your information, Todd and I are just friends."

"Hey, you guys," Brooke said, coming between us. "This is supposed to be a celebration, not a war."

"Who's fighting?" Amanda said, with an innocent

shrug. "Hey, I've got an idea. Maybe Brooke's sister can give us some boy advice."

I glared at Amanda and she glared right back.

What is that girl up to now? I wondered.

A couple of girls, including Amanda, walked over to Jewel who was sitting on the bench, writing on a clipboard. "Hey, who am I?" she said, looking up. "The love doctor?"

"I've got a question," Kristen piped up. "Is it smart to act dumb around boys?"

Jewel put her pen down. "Say that again?"

"It's like this," Kristen explained. "My cousin, Ashley, is the smartest kid in her grade nine class, but she acts like she can't add two plus two around her boyfriend."

Jewel rolled her eyes. "I know some girls who are like that. But the guys I hang out with don't like girls who act fake."

Amanda squeezed in next to Jewel. "How do you get a guy to like you?" she asked. "Someone in the room wants to know, but she is too shy to ask."

My ears started to burn. I nudged Yin. "What is her problem? Why won't she leave me alone?"

Yin pushed me away. "Shhh … I want to listen."

"First of all," Jewel said, "you gotta let the guy know that you like him. Find an excuse to talk to him but be yourself. Then, if he doesn't act interested, back off, forget him. He's not right for you."

Amanda didn't look convinced. "But … what if he is amazing?"

"Hey, this isn't about you and Todd," Yin whispered. "She's talking about Craig."

Jewel put the clipboard down. "Get over him, Amanda."

"Maybe if I wear make-up," she went on. "Maybe then he will notice me. Hey, Jewel, do guys like your nose ring?"

Jewel's eyes flashed. "Fine, don't listen to me."

Her answer put Amanda in a snit and she stomped off. Jewel reached for her coat and was about to leave.

"Come with me," Yin said, grabbing my arm. "Hurry, before she leaves!" She dragged me half-dressed over to Jewel and said, "We've got a question."

I poked her. "We?"

She ignored me. "How does a girl know when she is ready to date?"

Jewel's emerald eyes lit up. "Ever heard of a Smooch Test?"

I stepped away. "Get real!"

Yin pulled me back. "Tell us about this test."

"Yeah," someone called out, "We all wanna know!"

A few girls started making loud kissing noises. Next thing I knew, the whole team had gathered around us.

"Close your eyes," Jewel instructed. "Both of you."

"No way." I turned to leave, but was hemmed in by

a circle of girls.

Yin flapped her arms. "Bawk! Bawk!"

Okay, I know, I deserved that one.

Jewel laughed. "Come on, Maya, don't be a coward."

"Do it!" someone called out. Soon everyone joined in: "Do it! Do it! Do it!"

Brooke started dancing in her lace camisole and yellow ducky underwear. She was swinging her jersey over her head and singing, "Oh, baby, baby, kiss me."

That cracked me up something fierce. "Oh, all right," I said, laughing along.

Yin stood up on her toes. "Goody!"

"Close your eyes," Jewel said, "and relax."

Yin brought her heels back to the ground, and we both closed our eyes.

"Now," Jewel said, "imagine you are about to kiss some guy."

"Todd," Amanda whispered in the background.

I opened my eyes. "Forget it. This is stupid."

"Boo!" someone called out. "Maya failed the Smooch Test."

Rolling my eyes, I turned to Yin, getting ready to share a good laugh. Huh? What was with her? She was on her tiptoes gazing up with goo-goo eyes at some imaginary guy. Her lips were puckered. This was a Yin I had never seen before. My best friend had fallen in love, and she hadn't even told me.

"Who is that guy?" I demanded, pointing at the air.

She gave me a strange little smile. "Thomas Zhang." she said, as though the most beautiful words in the world had just slipped off her tongue.

"When did you meet him?"

She gave me that funny smile again. "Well, I haven't actually met him," she explained. "He's 15 and plays the cello in the community symphony orchestra." Her mouth dropped into a pout. "He is performing tonight, and I'm missing him because of hockey."

Jewel reached out, messing up Yin's hair. As always, every last strand fell back into place. "Sometimes it's more fun to dream about boys than to actually date them," she assured Yin.

As Jewel was leaving the dressing room, Coach arrived, her blue cape swooping behind her like wings.

"I have a few announcements," she said. "Practice is cancelled due to an Old Timers' hockey tournament. Our next game is Thursday night at 7:30." Her eyes searched the room and finally settled on me. I shifted uncomfortably on the bench. "Maya, you will be our goaltender."

I sat up with a jolt. I knew my time would come, but I wasn't ready. "Do I have to?" I whined.

She nodded. "It is your turn."

"But I ..."

"Don't bother," Yin said. "It's no use. Coach won't let you get out of it."

"Just watch me," I said, rising to the challenge. "There is no way I am going to be the goalie. Alone in the net, with the entire team depending on me … I'd get monster rash. And under all that goalie gear … it could be fatal."

Yin laughed. "No one has ever died of an itch."

"How do you know?" I said. "I bet someone did, and I bet it was a horrible, ugly …"

Just then, one of my teammates walked out the door, and I noticed Gram and Gramps waiting in the hall. I quickly gathered up my stuff and headed out the door.

13 "Eau de Moo" Perfume

On Monday morning the sun sparkled in a sapphire blue sky. It seemed like a perfect day, until I stepped outside. My breath filled the air with little white clouds.

Mr Pullen taught the class a unit on agriculture. He showed us the different types of farming in our area. He had posted charts and graphs all over the blackboard. It looked like the morning was going to be a real snoozer. In silent protest, I took out a pen and doodled pictures of cows on a piece of paper.

"What does a dairy farm produce?" Mr Pullen asked.

Craig raised his hand, enthusiastically pumping the air. "Manure," he said, with a big grin. "Mounds of cow pies."

I dropped my pen and joined in the laughter.

At this point, some teachers would send Craig into the hall, or, perhaps, to the office. Not Mr Pullen. He had his own form of punishment.

"Good answer, Craig," he said, his eyes dancing behind his glasses. Then he turned to the rest of the class and smiled. "We will come back to the subject of dairy farms in a few minutes. But right now, Craig has brought up a serious environmental issue: bovine excrement."

He went on to explain that manure can be a valuable resource. He told us it makes an excellent garden fertilizer. A few farmers have even converted it into electricity. No kidding! But when manure is not managed properly, it can cause big problems. Mr Pullen described how rain and melting snow wash manure straight into creeks and streams that flow into the lake where I swim. Pee-yew! All that moo-poo talk nauseated me. By recess, I was glad to get outside.

Amanda and I were barely speaking, but since she was hanging with Brooke, and Brooke was hanging with Yin and me, we were still all together. Craig and Todd walked past us, tossing a basketball back and forth.

"Hey, Craig," Amanda called. "Wait up!"

Craig whirled around on his heels. His eyes focused in on the thick, black eye-liner she had applied that morning. "Ew, what did you do? You look like a raccoon."

Amanda's head jerked back, as if she had been hit with a fist, and I could see the hurt in her eyes. But just as quickly, her face hardened, and she came back swinging — only she wasn't aiming for Craig.

"Hey, Todd," she said, playfully. "Guess what Maya did last night?"

Remembering my winning goal, I flushed with pride.

He shrugged. "I give."

Amanda glanced over at me. "Should I tell?"

"I don't care," I said, but secretly I was hoping she would.

Giggling, she stuck out her lips cooing, "Smooch … smooch."

There was a stunned silence.

Suddenly I cried out: "Don't you dare! That's private."

"Quit it, Amanda," Yin warned. "You are not funny."

"Don't worry," Amanda said. "I won't tell, if you don't want me to … but how about we get Todd to take the Smooch Test?"

Todd's ears burned red. He looked like he wanted to run away.

Amanda wouldn't let up. "I have an even better idea. Since Maya is right here, Todd doesn't need to pretend. How about the real thing? Come on, Todd — plant a wet one on Maya's lips. Let's see if you really are the man of her dreams."

"Stop it, Amanda," Brooke warned. "You're going too far."

But it was too late. Without a word, Todd walked away and Craig followed.

Amanda shrugged. "Looks like Todd failed the test, too."

"How could you?" I screamed at her. "You are so mean."

I didn't stick around for an answer. I ran off, and Yin came after me, calling, "Maya, wait up!"

"Are you okay?" she asked, when she caught up.

"No," I said, wiping away the tears. "Amanda ruined everything ... on purpose. Now I'll never be able to face Todd."

"Amanda is the one who messed up," Yin said. "She's jealous ... because Todd likes you, and you don't even have to try."

"Yeah, well I can't help it if Craig ignores her. But you know what — I don't care. She's not my friend anymore."

"I don't blame you," Yin said. "That's no way to treat a friend."

* * *

After school, I took the bus straight home. Dad had left a note on the kitchen table reminding me that he was working until seven and would bring home a late supper. Actually, I was glad to be alone because I had to make a private call.

After grabbing an oatmeal cookie, I stopped to check the hockey schedule on the fridge. Thursday night we were scheduled to play the Gators, the team that had crushed us in the first game. I remembered how the Gators had laughed at us last time, and called me the winger who couldn't play hockey.

We'd show those reptiles. And I would do my part to ensure a victory. Locating Coach's phone number, I began to dial. After five rings, someone picked up: "Hello."

I immediately recognized Mrs Duval's voice. "Uh … h-hi," I stumbled. "This is Maya Sanchez."

"Why, yes, of course," she said, cheerfully. "How are you, Maya?"

"Uh … not very well," I said, in a sickly voice. "I have a bad skin p-problem. It's called urticaria."

"Oh my," she said, sounding concerned. "I hope it's not serious."

"It's a rash," I explained. "I'm really sorry, but I won't be able to play hockey this Thursday."

"Oh dear, that does put me in a pickle. You are supposed to be our goaltender. Is there any chance you will feel better?"

"No," I said, firmly. "In fact, I'll get worse."

She sighed. "Perhaps I can convince Danielle to take your place. Well, thank you for phoning, Maya. And I do hope you feel better soon."

I hadn't actually told a lie. I knew if I played in net,

I would get urticaria. It was better for the team that I pulled out early. Even so … Mrs Duval had been really nice … and poor Danielle, having to be goalie again. Okay, so I felt terrible! But what choice did I have?

Anyway, I couldn't dwell on it because I had an even bigger problem: Amanda.

Right then and there, I made a decision: I was not an ant, and I was not going to let her stomp on me anymore. I was going to fight back.

14 No Way Out

The next morning I was waiting in the drop-off zone when Todd filed off the bus. He was wearing a new grey and yellow snowboard jacket.

"Nice coat," I called out.

He pushed past me and kept walking.

"Guess what?" I said, running to catch up. "I scored the other night. My first goal. And I used that neat little tip-in you showed me."

He stopped and turned. "Really? That's awesome!" And just like that, we were buds again.

Standing by the buses, I gave him a quick rundown of the game. He got totally into it, and so did I — especially the part about my winning goal. But as soon as we stopped talking about hockey, he got uptight again. I had been wrong. We were not cool.

This is hopeless, I told myself. I contemplated heading over to the schoolyard to find my friends. Then I pictured Amanda and thought again. Even though my stomach was tied up in a knot, I decided to give it one more shot. "About yesterday ..." I said.

He cut me off. "What was Amanda trying to prove?"

"I'm not sure," I said. "But this is what happened. After the game, the team was goofing around in the locker room. Brooke's older sister, Jewel, was doing silly tests to see who was ready to date. I think Amanda wanted you to know that I failed. But it was just a joke ..." I looked away, feeling foolish.

"So ... what's the big deal?" he said. "I'm not ready to date, either. I'll have to toughen up a lot before I ask a girl out."

"Huh? What do you mean?"

"Just that you have taught me something," he said, with a straight face. "Girls can be dangerous. I am limping, my right ear is ringing, and as for my nose ..." He put his hands over his face and made a loud crack.

I positioned my hands for a karate chop. "Hey, you wanna see dangerous?"

Next thing I knew, he was cowering down on the sidewalk, begging, "Please don't hurt me."

Kids gathered around, whispering.

"Quit joking," I said. "Get up, Todd! I mean it! You're embarrassing me!" He didn't budge, so I leaned over to haul him up. At the same time, he stood ... fast. Our heads collided. I saw stars — pretty flashing lights. Then we both went down.

"Fight!" a little kid yelled, and a crowd came running. Todd and I lay on the ground, moaning and laughing.

★ ★ ★

After school, I took the city bus to the Linton Heights Arena. I couldn't wait to try some jumps and spins. As I entered the building, Natasha came running up to me.

"The pre-school skaters will be arriving soon," she said. "Until then, you can have the ice all to yourself. Have you been stretching — practicing the routine I taught you?"

"Yes," I replied honestly.

She ordered me to her office. "Before I allow you to skate, I must see that you are prepared. Show me."

Sitting with a straight back on the carpeted floor, I straddled my legs and slowly lowered my chest down to the floor.

"Very good," Natasha said, clapping. "All loosey-goosey. Now … start at the beginning."

After I had gone through my full stretching routine, Natasha sent me to the dressing room where I changed into blue leggings and a pink sweater. When I glided onto the ice, I had to think … toe pick … heel. But it didn't take long to feel comfortable in my white skates. All those years of figure skating couldn't be erased by a few months of hockey.

By the time the pre-school skaters hit the ice, I had practiced a few easy jumps and spins. I was thinking about attempting the double Axel when Natasha introduced me to my students. I was supposed to teach the kids how to glide, but I spent most of the time picking them up off the ice. After that we played followed-the-leader. I would start skating and they would follow in a line like ducklings trailing after the mama duck. As I weaved my group in a large figure eight, I skated close to the boards. That's when I noticed Mrs Duval peering through the glass. With a start, I remembered: I was supposed to be sick.

Immediately, I veered away.

Maybe she didn't see me, I told myself. And with any luck, she will be gone by the end of the practice.

A few minutes later, as I skated off the ice, Mrs Duval was still standing by the gate. I had been caught.

"Hi, Coach," I said, faking a smile. "What are you doing here?"

She held up her hockey skates. "The adult skate. I need plenty of practice to keep up with you girls."

"Well … have fun," I said, attempting a quick getaway.

"Hold on," she said. "I see that you're feeling fine. Can I count on you to be the goaltender at tomorrow night's game?"

"No!" I blurted. "I can't!"

"But Maya … your skating is strong; you look healthy."

"I won't be okay by tomorrow," I said, then added, "Not if I'm goalie."

She eyed me closely. "Maya," she said, at last. "I do not understand."

Slumping against the boards, I explained, "It's weird — whenever I get really nervous, little red bumps pop up all over my body. They are itchy and prickly at the same time. It happens when I have to say a speech in front of the class or figure skate in front of a crowd … and it will happen if I am stuck in a net with the rest of the team depending on me."

A warm smile softened Coach's face. "These nervous feelings you describe are rather common," she assured me. "In drama class we call it stage fright. It's okay to feel nervous, Maya, but it is not okay to be so afraid that you won't even try."

"But, Coach …"

She raised a hand to silence my protest. "Before a performance, my drama students do something that helps them feel more confident on stage. I think it might help you too. Can you come to the arena early on Thursday?"

"Um … I'm not sure if …"

"I will pick you up myself," she said, before I could finish.

Coach was smart — she had figured out all the

angles. There was no way out. I was doomed to play in goal against the first place team.

15 Defending the Nest

After an early supper, I stood by the front window keeping a look-out for Coach's car. Dad came over and put his big arm around me. "You'll be fine, Maya. I will be watching from the bleachers, cheering you on. No matter what happens tonight, you are a winner where it counts." He touched his heart. At the same time, I reached down my neck and touched Bela.

"I'll be okay, Dad," I assured him.

Just then, a red sports car pulled into my driveway.

"Adios!" Dad called, as I ran out the door.

Coach squeezed my equipment into the little trunk, and I crawled in the backseat next to Danielle.

"What is your mother going to do to me?" I whispered, anxiously.

She shrugged. "Beats me. But I wouldn't want to be you."

I stared at her wide-eyed.

"I'm so glad you're the goalie tonight," she went

on. "Otherwise, Mom would make me play in net again. Believe me, once was enough."

Talking to Danielle made me want to jump out of that car and run for my life.

At the community centre, Coach took Danielle and me to the all-purpose room. "Ready, Maya," she said, pointing to the blue carpet. "I want you to lie flat on your back and close your eyes."

I planted my feet firmly on the floor. "Why? What are you going to do?"

"Just listen," she said, calmly, "and do as I say."

I trusted Coach but …

"You may stop at any time if you are uncomfortable," she assured me.

I glanced over at Danielle. She was leaning against the wall, laughing into her coat sleeve. Smirking, I slunk down on the carpet and closed my eyes.

"Begin by breathing in … nice and deep," Coach said in a soothing voice. "Now, exhale slowly … all the way. Good, Maya. Breathe in … and out … in … and out …."

As if I had to be taught to breathe! This was easy … and useless. The whole time, I could hear Danielle in the background making strange choking sounds. I imagined her stuffing her sleeve down her throat to keep from laughing.

"Try to relax, Maya," Coach said. "Now, as you breathe in, I want you say to yourself 'I can' … and then, slowly breathe out all your negative thoughts.

"Wait! Is this hypnotism, cuz, like, I won't …"

"No," Coach said firmly. "I am simply trying to teach you the power of positive thinking. It can work if you let it. Ready now, breathe in 'I can' … Keep breathing. Allow only positive thoughts to enter your mind and let go of all the negative energy."

Something was happening to me, that's for sure. My stomach began to twitch like it was filled with jumping beans. Then it started to ripple. I tried desperately to hold myself together, that's when the tidal wave hit.

I exploded, laughing my guts out. Danielle burst out at the same time. We were howling so hard, we started crying. I struggled to get myself under control. Slowly, I managed to stop laughing and was sitting on the carpet gulping for air, when Danielle let out a loud pig snort. My insides began to heave and I fell back on the carpet laughing. All the while, Coach just stood there with a strange smile on her face. She didn't say a word until our laughter finally subsided. Then she quietly said, "Laughing is a wonderful form of relaxation. Keep it up, girls. Let go of all the tension."

Suddenly, it wasn't funny anymore.

Coach directed Danielle to the carpet. "You might as well join Maya. She is having trouble concentrating knowing that you're watching."

"I'll be quiet," Danielle promised.

"Down you go," Coach ordered. "This will benefit both of you."

Reluctantly, she joined me on the floor. It's a good thing because I wouldn't have wanted to be alone when things got really strange.

"Now," Coach said, "I want you both to imagine that you are eagles — proud and determined birds of prey. Maya, you are the mother eagle watching over your nest. Tonight you will defend the nest against a swarm of attacking alligators, predators that love to eat baby eagles. Danielle, you will swoop down on those Gators, keeping them out of the Eagles' territory. Together, you girls shall defend the nest."

Coach sure got dramatic. Still, by the time she was finished, I almost believed the net was a nest and that I had eagle blood coursing through my veins.

With only twenty minutes until game time, Danielle and I hurried to the dressing room. On the way, she said, "I am so sorry, Maya. My mother is totally embarrassing. That bit about alligators attacking the eagle's nest — I don't think so — unless alligators can fly!"

"It's okay," I said, laughing. "Actually, I think your mom is a good coach. She's just got her own unique style."

In the dressing room, Jewel was waiting for me with the bag of goalie equipment. She helped to dress me, turning me into a blimp. To my surprise, I actually felt calm — ready to defend the nest … net — whatever! Coach's positive thinking seemed to be working. There was only one thing bothering me now — Brooke and Amanda kept whispering and looking over at me. I tried to ignore them, until Brooke nudged Amanda right off the bench. She hesitated, and then walked over to me.

"I — uh — just want to say that I'm sorry," she said, rocking on her skate blades. "Oh, yeah, and I broke up with Craig."

"Broke up?" I couldn't believe my ears. "Craig hardly ever talked to you."

"I think that was part of the problem with our relationship," Amanda explained. "Anyway, he was making me act crazy. And I feel really bad about what I did to you. So I did something to try and make-up."

I sat straight up and demanded, "What did you do?"

"I brought Todd to the game tonight — for you!"

"What? No! You didn't!" I started to sweat. Todd is here — to watch me!"

Amanda's mouth fell open. "But … I thought …"

With a gulp, I inhaled a big "I can't." And then, it happened: my skin began to itch. Panicking, I threw my goalie gloves on the bench.

Danielle ran out in the hall, yelling, "Mom you'd better get in here. Fast!"

16 A Dream of My Own

Coach came dashing into the locker room as I was ditching the goalie pads. "Maya," she said, breathing hard. "What's wrong?"

I slumped over on the bench, dropping my head in my hands. "I can't go out there."

Coach called Jewel over. "Take the team outside," she instructed. "Have them line up, ready to go on the ice. When the Zamboni clears the ice, take them through their warm-up. I will join you as soon as I am able."

Coach didn't say another word until the locker room had cleared out. Then she sat next to me and spoke softly. "Maya, what are you afraid of?"

I fixed my eyes on floor and scratched, good and hard. "Messing up, I guess … and looking dumb … and making the team lose …"

"Hold everything," she said. "One person cannot win or lose a hockey game. You are part of our team.

We win together, or we lose together."

I reached into my hockey bag, searching for my anti-itch spray. When I found the little bottle, I aimed down my jersey and let go a blast.

"Better?" she asked.

"Not really. I don't think the spray actually works."

"It's okay," she said, patting my knee. "I understand. I won't force you to go out there." She stood and headed for the door. "I've got to find a volunteer … fast."

It had taken a lot of convincing, but Coach finally saw things my way. I wouldn't have to take my turn in goal. I should have been happy. But I wasn't. I was angry — at myself. "Wait!" I waved her back. "I'll do it."

Coach stopped by the door and regarded me. "Are you sure? Don't go out there because I put pressure on you."

"I'm okay," I assured her. "I just got freaked."

By the time I skated onto the rink, my team was sitting on the bench and our mascot sat perched by the glass. Dad was standing up on a bleacher, his eyes scanning the arena, looking worried. When he saw me, he waved and sat down next to Natasha. Huh? What was she doing at the game? Then I realized she was sitting next to Mr Neal and they were holding hands. What the — ? Amanda hadn't said a word — then again, I hadn't exactly been speaking to her lately. At first, I couldn't find Todd, then I spotted him leaning against the boards. He gave me a thumbs-up as I skated past.

Stay cool, I told myself.

The Gators did their best to intimidate us, beginning with a cheer they had invented especially for our team:

We're mean, we're green,
Nothing in between.
And what do we eat?
Eagles taste sweet ...
Surrender! You're gonna lo-o-o-se!

As I skated to the net, my rash was on a prickly assault. And it was bound to get worse under the heavy goalie pads. Oh, how I needed to scratch or wiggle or scream! Trying to ignore it, I did a few stretches to loosen up.

"Mom," I said, moments before the game. "I know you understand. This one is for me."

The ref blew the whistle. Right away, the Gators gained control of the puck. I crouched down in the goalie stance, waiting and wiggling. Their centre brought the puck down the ice. She zoomed into our zone, deking out Danielle. I kept my eyes trained on her as she skated toward the goal crease. Next thing I knew, it was just the two of us — one-on-one. Her stick pulled back. Wham! She fired the puck high at the left corner of the net. I shot my glove in the air and felt a thump. Turning my hand over, I looked in amazement at the puck sitting in my glove. A line of Eagles swooped past me, giving me high-fives.

The Gators were hungry for a goal. In less than a minute, they were back on the attack. Yin was busy at the boards trying to dig the puck away from their winger. She finally popped it loose, but another Gator beat her to the puck. The girl slammed a low shot on net. Dropping down into a butterfly save, I felt the puck deflect off my shin. I was starting to get up, when I heard someone yell, "Rebound!"

A Gator jabbed at the puck with her stick. It went dribbling slowly up to the net. I was out of position and couldn't get back fast enough. Desperately, I took a dive, smothering the puck under my body.

By the end of the first period the score was 0-0. My itch had vanished; it had been replaced by an intense fever — game fever.

At the start of the second period, Amanda wrestled a big Gator for control of the puck. After a long struggle, she managed to kick the puck to Kristen who glided in close to the Gators' net. Winding up, Kristen took a shot, but it was blocked by their goalie.

Before I knew it, the action was back in our end. A green jersey was closing in with the puck. She crossed over the blue line. Her stick went back. Smack! The slap shot was hard and deadly accurate. With no time to think, I dove through the air, landing on my side, with the puck buried safely under me. The Gators kept attacking, one after another, and I loved it. At the end of the second period the score was still 0-0. And it stayed that way until the last minute of the game.

Twenty-seven seconds appeared on the clock.

Yin fired the puck up the ice to Kristen. A Gator got there first and passed it down the ice to her teammate. But Amanda was faster, skating in between the two girls and intercepting the puck. In a flash, she took off toward the Gator's net.

Fifteen … fourteen … thirteen …

A familiar voice started yelling, "Go, Amanda, go!" My heart sank. We had been so close, but now it was all over. Amanda would never score with her dad on her back. The stick fell from my hand.

But wait — something was different. There was a new tone in his voice. Mr Neal wasn't trying to coach Amanda — he was cheering her on. The crowd joined in: "Go, Amanda, go!"

Eight … seven … six …

Amanda flew across the blue line. She weaved around one Gator and out-skated another. Smack! She let loose a low, hard shot. The puck went hurtling forward, popped over the goalie's glove, and dropped into the goal.

The buzzer rang. The game was over. 1-0: Eagles.

Amanda skated the length of the rink and embraced me, pulling me down on the ice.

"We did it!" she cheered.

"Yahoo!" I cried. Then I braced myself as the whole team came swooping down on us.

"Are you still mad at me?" Amanda asked, as we lay pinned in the bottom of the heap.

"I'm not sure," I said, shouting above the players. "Are you really over Craig?"

"Totally and completely. Hey, if I tell you a secret, promise you won't tell anyone?"

I pushed someone's elbow out of my neck. "I am getting crushed and you want to tell secrets!"

She drew close. "I think Matt Gagnon likes me. Maybe I could volunteer with you at the Linton Heights' Arena. That way I could be close to him."

Oh no, I thought, banging my helmet on the ice, here we go again.

When we finally stood up, I waved at Dad. At the same time, Amanda grabbed me from behind. She was pointing at her dad and Natasha. "When you said Natasha would take care of my dad I didn't think you meant …"

I laughed. "Hey, I didn't. But don't worry, Natasha is cool. You'll like her."

Amanda rolled her eyes. "I hope so."

When the teams lined up to shake hands, Yin skated up behind me. "Now you've done it," she said. "You'll have to be our permanent goalie."

I smacked gloves with her. "Right on!"

"So …" she said, "did you and Amanda make up?"

Brooke poked her head between us. "She really is sorry, you know."

I just shook my head. "How can I stay mad after our amazing win?"

Yin laughed. "Maybe she's finally learned that friends come first."

"Let's hope so," I said, as I skated off the ice.

Coach stopped me by the gate. "I am proud of you, Maya," she said. "You faced your fears and won."

"It was pretty cool," I said. "The whole team played awesome."

Coach beamed. "Yes, they certainly did. I knew this team would soar one day."

"Yeah," I said. "It's like we finally found our wings."

Oh, no, I was talking like a bird.

"Coach," I said, "I got pretty lucky tonight. But if I'm going to be a decent goalie, I'll need to learn a lot more. Do you think that Brett Holloway would …"

"I'll talk to him before class tomorrow," she said. "See if I can get him to help out a fellow goalie."

"Thanks," I said, "for everything."

"My pleasure," she said. "We rookies have to stick together." She left to congratulate the rest of the players.

I was pumped. For the first time in my life, I was doing something for me. I had found my dream in the most unlikely place. Nothing could stop me now for I, Maya Sanchez, was a goalie.

Spanish Vocabulary List

Adios – Good-bye
Amigos – Friends
Arriba- Get up! Come on!
Ay! - Oh, dear! (sighing, moaning gesture)
Bueno – Good
Buenos dias – Good morning.
Chino – Curly
Chiquita – feminine: Little one – familiar
Delicioso – Delicious
Fiesta – a celebration
Loco – Crazy
Magnifico – Magnificent
No importa – It doesn't matter
No esta bien – That's no good.
Pronto – quick, prompt.
Senorita – Young lady, Miss
Si – Yes

Sources

Just Enough Spanish, National Textbook Co., U.S.A., 1983

Internet: Yahooligans Reference American Heritage Spanish Dictionary
El Chino – Sp./American: The Chinaman, Sp./Mexican: The Curly one
See eg.
Site:.qconline.com/progress98/dining/prchinos.html
(Taste the old country at Chinos)

Hockey

www.ask jeeves.com Hockey Canada Rules

Figure Skating

Morrissey, Peter and James Young, Figure Skating School, Firefly Books, Canada, 1997. (Great reference for technique)

www.goecities.com/unseen skate/news/skaterarticles/02/tento watch.html

Other books you'll enjoy in the Sports Stories series

Ice Hockey

❑ *The Enforcer* by Bill Swan

In this sequel to *Deflection*, Jake Henry plays goalie for his hockey team. When the team's coach moves away, Jake's grandfather steps in to fill the role. Can the team adapt to Grandpa P.J's old-school methods?

❑ *Deflection! by Bill Swan*

Jake and his two best friends play road hockey together and are members of the same league team. But some personal rivalries and interference from Jake's three all-too-supportive grandfathers start to create tension among the players.

❑ *Misconduct* by Beverly Scudamore

Matthew has always been a popular student and hockey player. But after an altercation with a tough kid named Dillon at hockey camp, Matt finds himself number one on the bully's hit list.

❑ *Roughing by Lorna Schultz Nicholson*

Josh is off to an elite hockey camp for the summer, where his roommate, Peter, is skilled enough to give Kevin, the star junior player, some serious competition, creating trouble on and off the ice.

❑ *Home Ice* by Beatrice Vandervelde

Leigh Aberdeen is determined to win the hockey championship with a new, all girls team, the Chinooks.

❑ *Against the Boards* by Lorna Schultz Nicholson

Peter has made it onto an AAA Bantam team and is now playing hockey in Edmonton. But this shy boy from the Northwest Territories is having a hard time adjusting to his new life.

❑ *Delaying the Game* by Lorna Schultz Nicholson

When Shane comes along, Kaleigh finds herself unsure whether she can balance hockey, her friendships, and this new dating-life.